COWARD OF SAND CREEK

COWARD OF SAND CREEK

JOHN LEGG

THORNDIKE PRESS
A part of Gale, a Cengage Company

Copyright © 2021 John Legg.
Thorndike Press, a part of Gale, a Cengage Company.

Thorndike Press® Large Print Hardcover Western.
The text of this Large Print edition is unabridged.
Other aspects of the book may vary from the original edition.
Set in 16 pt. Plantin.

LIBRARY OF CONGRESS CIP DATA ON FILE.
CATALOGUING IN PUBLICATION FOR THIS BOOK
IS AVAILABLE FROM THE LIBRARY OF CONGRESS.

ISBN-13: 979-8-8857-8285-2 (hardcover alk. paper)

Published in 2022 by arrangement with Wolfpack Publishing LLC.

Printed in Mexico
Print Number : 1   Print Year : 2023

AUTHOR'S NOTE

The massacre at Sand Creek did occur on Nov. 29, 1864. However, since this is a work of fiction, I have changed the timing of the actual events. It is unlikely that the desecration of bodies began so early in the assault. The offensive lasted about eight hours, and while the depredations most certainly began before the end, I don't think they began this early in the day. Captain Silas Soule and Lieutenant Joseph Cramer are real figures and did indeed keep their companies out of the assault (and Soule was shot to death in April 1865). The only other real person is Major Scott Anthony, who has a small mention. That said, the main character and all the other characters and events after Chapter 6 of Coward at Sand Creek are fictitious, as is the timing of some events surrounding Sand Creek.

CHAPTER 1

Chase Tanner was not a squeamish man, but the horrors he saw before him stunned him with their chilling wickedness. He could not believe men — supposedly civilized men fighting those they called savages — could have acted in such a depraved manner. The men had savagely slaughtered anyone who crossed their path: men, warriors or not, women, including those who were with child, and worse, children, some barely able to walk, beaten, their heads pounded with gun butts and rocks, or shot as they stood screaming in fright. And the depraved acts committed on the bodies of the dead or the almost dead horrified him: the slicing of fetuses out of dead women, the carving off of private parts from both men and women, the taking of scalps, and the hacking off of fingers and ears to snatch rings or earrings.

Along with more than six hundred other soldiers, he had charged down the hill on this bitter November morning into the sleeping Cheyenne and Arapaho camp on Sand Creek.

He had been expecting a battle with armed and strong warriors. Instead, he had found peaceful men, mostly old, and innocent women, and children. He and the other members of the Colorado Militia were sick of the Cheyennes raiding and killing throughout the plains of the Colorado Territory, so he and the other men were primed to chastise the Indians. To deal them a blow strong enough to keep them from resuming their depredations.

He had not wanted to believe what he had heard at Fort Lyon — that these were peaceful Indians under the protection of the regular Army, or at least of some of the officers at the post. But as he raced his horse down the hill, firing a few times at armed warriors, it slowly became clear that those words were true. He reined in his horse and sat for some minutes, appalled by the depravity of men he knew as neighbors.

Tanner slid off his horse, his rifle falling from his hand when it banged against his saddle, and raced to where two soldiers, men he didn't know well from another company, had just killed a woman and laughed as they cut out her unborn child.

One tossed the fetus to the ground, and the other dashed its brains out with a pistol butt. The two men bent to remove her womanhood. He slammed into both, bowling them over, then kicked one in the face and pounded a fist into the other's cheek several times.

"What the hell's wrong with you, Chase?" the one he had kicked asked in surprise and irritation.

"Animals," he muttered. It took all his willpower to not kill these men. He kicked each one in the temple, knocking them unconscious. Breathing heavily, he stood a few moments, then charged another soldier, a thick-bodied dimwit named Baxter who was about to shoot a child he figured was no older than three. He slammed his two fists clasped together into the side of the soldier's head.

As the man dropped, Tanner looked around with wild eyes, searching for more chances to stop the carnage. He quickly realized he could not save many of the Cheyennes, and he could not stop all the militiamen. Still, he had to do something.

He raced to where three soldiers held a weakly struggling old man down as one cut through the buckskin strap to which his breechclout and leggings were attached. The men were laughing as they exposed the old man's privates. The knife-wielding soldier, a gangly young man named Don Atkins, grabbed the aging warrior's scrotum and penis and, grinning at his companions, started to bring the blade down on them. Tanner, who had grabbed a fallen rifle, pulled the trigger without aiming, but the weapon was empty. He used it as a club instead, smashing the buttstock into Atkins' head. The man fell.

The two other soldiers, middle-aged townsmen named Dexter Cobb and Aaron Pitts, turned and started to draw their pistols but stopped in shock when they saw it was a fellow soldier who had attacked them. That was all the time Tanner needed to bash the two in the face and send them crashing to the ground, unconscious or nearly so.

"Run!" he shouted above the bedlam around him, looking at the old warrior. "Go!"

The old man staggered up and wobbled off, heedless of his nudity from the waist down as his breechclout fell.

Tanner watched helplessly as a bullet exploded through the Cheyenne's head, spinning him around before he fell dead.

Tanner was numb from seeing the carnage

and wickedness around him, and after several more moments, he could not move. He became aware of a rifle-wielding man he vaguely thought was a half-breed taking aim at him, but he could do nothing. He was frozen in place, dazed by what was happening before his eyes. He realized he did not care if the man shot him. It would keep him from having to watch more of this sinfulness.

But then the man lowered his rifle, jerked his head once to indicate that Tanner should flee, then disappeared into the smoke and mist.

Tanner finally broke out of his funk. He grabbed the reins of the nearest horse, neither knowing nor caring whether it was his own. He leaped on and galloped up the hill, knocking over a pair of soldiers who were shooting at a group of fleeing women. He reached one company that had stayed put, its commander refusing to have his men join the madness.

Also running up the hill were a few Cheyennes, fear on their faces. The soldiers allowed them through. More would follow.

"Permission to join your company, Captain?" Tanner asked as he stopped in front of Captain Silas Soule.

"Unwilling to fight the savages, eh?" Soule

11

responded with a tight, humorless grin.

"I'll fight savages anytime, anywhere. This ain't fighting savages. This is a massacre of women and children and old men. No glory in it, only shame, and no need for it."

"Your name?"

"Corporal Chase Tanner, Sir."

"Take your place next to Sergeant Ralston."

"Yes, sir." Tanner saluted, then rode up and turned his horse to sit side by side with the company's top sergeant. From the brief look he got as he took his position, Tanner thought all but a few of the enlisted men agreed with Soule's decision not to take part in the fight, though he thought no decent man would call what was happening a fight.

Ralston leaned toward Tanner and said quietly, "I saw what you did down there."

Tanner looked sharply at him. He could see nothing in the eyes of the sergeant to indicate whether what he had said was a compliment or a condemnation.

It was a long, bitter morning as the men of D Company of the 1st Colorado Calvary sat watching the horrors along the creek. Cheyennes and Arapahos, young and old, male and female, all screaming in terror, continued to trickle through the ranks of the cavalrymen.

12

Just after noon, Soule's commander, Major Scott Anthony, assigned D Company to watch over wounded soldiers and guard the Army's supplies. Among the wounded were several of the men Tanner had attacked. Two of them, the first two he had stopped from their deviltry, whom Tanner learned were Emmet Barton and Sid Landis, staggered to their feet and reached for their pistols, but Ralston and a pair of other soldiers disarmed them.

"Just watch yourself, boy," Barton said to Tanner.

"Gonna shoot me in the back like you did those women and kids?"

"They're murderin' savages."

"No, they're women and young 'uns, and maybe a few old men. You and the rest of your ilk are the murderin' savages."

"Just wait 'til the colonel hears about you," Landis said.

"I lost all respect for Colonel Chivington at dawn today." Tanner felt the anger rising in him.

"Colonel Chivington is gonna make sure you and all the cowardly bastards under Indian-lovin' Soule and that other lily-livered officer — Cramer, is it? — are shot. None of you deserve to be called members of the Colorado Cavalry."

13

"After what I saw here today, I'm proud of the fact that I'm not included with devils like you. I . . ."

"That's enough, Corporal," Sgt. Miles Ralston, the top noncom, said.

Again, Tanner wasn't sure if he was being warned off in a friendly manner as if Ralston thought the wounded men were beneath contempt, or an unfriendly one as if Ralston agreed with the two and was ordering Tanner to leave them alone or else.

"Besides, time to saddle up again. Major Anthony's sending D Company to escort a supply train downriver."

"What for?"

"You been in the Army long enough now to know that men like us don't question an officer's commands."

"Sometimes we do," Tanner said quietly.

A hint of a smile cracked Ralston's face. "Reckon you're right, but this one doesn't go against the grain, though maybe it goes against common sense."

After a few days, D Company returned to Fort Lyon. They had avoided skirmishes with bands of angry Cheyennes and Arapahos, traveling through the freezing cold and a snowstorm.

At Fort Lyon, Tanner approached Captain

Soule. "If I might have a word, Sir?"

"Of course, Corporal. What's on your mind?"

"Officially, I's still assigned to M Company under Lieutenant Whittemore. I'd like to transfer to D Company, Sir."

"You'll be mustering out soon."

"I know that, but I'd rather do so as a member of D Company after what's gone on."

"I can certainly understand that."

"That is, Sir, if it won't cause you any trouble."

Soule grinned. "To be honest, Corporal, I believe I'm already in a heap of trouble. A little more won't hurt, I expect. Lieutenant Whittemore might object, but I outrank him, of course, so it won't be a problem. I'll come up with a reason for the official paperwork, though I figure he'll know the real reason."

"Yes, Sir."

"Anything else, Corporal?"

Tanner hesitated before finally saying, "I believe you'll be risking your career — and more — by protesting what happened at . . ."

"Dismissed, Corporal," Soule snapped.

"If you'll let me finish, Sir?"

Soule took a deep breath and let it out,

then nodded.

"If I'm wrong, then it'll be me in a heap of trouble. If I'm right, well, all I wanted to say is that if you need me to support you in any way over this affair, all you need to do is ask. I'll be happy to testify should an inquiry be made or anything else."

"Such a view is foolhardy."

"I hate to contradict an officer, Captain, but I disagree. What you did — or rather, didn't do — at Sand Creek took courage, and I respect that. I was sick at what I saw there, and I was glad I participated for only a few minutes. I'm mighty thankful too that you gave me a place in your company. Lest you think I'm a coward, which I don't think you do," Tanner said, raising his hand to stop any protest, "I'm not. I'll fight Indians anytime, anywhere with all I got. Killin' helpless women and kids ain't Indian fightin'. I believe you feel the same."

Soule stared at Tanner for some moments, making the corporal squirm a little. Then the officer said, "I do. If there is any kind of inquiry, and I hope there is, it most assuredly will be officers only testifying. But if they want to hear from noncoms or enlisted men, I'll remember this talk." He smiled. "Now you're really dismissed, Corporal. I have work to do."

16

"Yes, Sir. Thank you, Sir." Tanner saluted and left.

"Yes, Sir. Thank you, Sir," Tanner saluted and left.

CHAPTER 2

The 1st Colorado Volunteer Cavalry rode triumphantly into Denver just before Christmas. By and large, the men were greeted as heroes. The soldiers, whose enlistments were to end very soon, proudly displayed their grisly trophies — scalps, fingers, ears, genitalia both male and female, and breasts — and those not so grisly like buffalo robes, war shirts, rings, and other jewelry.

Captain Soule had stayed at Fort Lyon, so D Company and M Company were led into Denver by Lieutenant Joseph Cramer. The unit was looked upon with a little less favor once word got out that the two companies had not participated in the battle, as Colonel Chivington referred to it.

Despite it being so close to Christmas, Tanner was in no mood to celebrate. Visions of the slaughter still plagued him. He brooded over a bottle of whiskey in a room at a boarding house, thinking about what he had done and wondering what he should do with his life now.

He wasn't sure he wanted to stay here in Colorado Territory, but he did not know where else he could go. He supposed he could return to his hometown in Pennsylvania and go back to working on the docks of the Delaware River near Philadelphia, but his relationship with his family was not the best, and that life did not appeal to him.

He didn't know what he would do here, though. It had been a long trip to get where he was. He had still been a young man working the docks when word had come that gold had been discovered at some stream called Cherry Creek near a mountain someone had named Pike's Peak. The possibility of riches intrigued him and the desire for wealth began to eat at him, finally pushing him to decide to seek his fortune.

Though he had been helping his family monetarily, he had lived frugally, so he had some money saved up. When he announced his attention to leave, the trouble with the family started. They wanted to know if he would send money to help support them as he had been doing. They were not poor by any means, though certainly not rich, but his help had provided them with extras — better food, a few luxuries, and such — and their greed offended him. No one seemed to care about his well-being or his future, just that his monetary help was going away.

Disgruntled, he packed his few possessions in a knapsack, bought a guidebook for a dime, and made his way to St. Joseph, Missouri, by rail, stage, and boat. There he bought a horse, a mule, and as many supplies as the mule could carry. Though he didn't really know how to use them, he also bought a muzzle-loading rifle and a cap-and-ball Colt revolver, along with powder, lead, and percussion caps. A few days later, he set off for Pike's Peak with a dozen other hopeful prospectors and a guide they had hired named Buck Waterman.

Three and a half weeks out, he shot his first buffalo. He quickly learned it was not easy and that it was even harder to butcher it through the thick hide. He also learned, however, that the meat was succulent, better than anything he had ever eaten.

Several days later, he met his first Indians when half a dozen warriors — Pawnees, he learned later — rode up and demanded "gifts" for traveling across their land. Waterman took some twists of tobacco from a sack hanging from his saddle horn and tossed them to the leader of the Pawnees. "That's all you get, boys," the long-ago mountain man said.

"Want more. Powder, lead too."

"Go to hell. Now be on your way and be thankful I'm so kindly as to give you what I did."

Tanner and his two nearest companions looked at each other in worry. "What in hell's he doing?" Tanner muttered.

White-faced in fear, the travelers watched as Waterman argued with the Indians.

Suddenly, the Pawnee leader pulled up alongside the guide and swung a war club at the man's head. Waterman shifted out of the way, and the stone head of the weapon glanced off his shoulder. The guide drew his pistol and shot the warrior, then fired twice more and hit two others, though he did not kill either of them.

"Shoot, goddammit!" Waterman roared as an arrow hit him in the chest.

Four of the travelers managed to get their pistols out and began firing, mostly wildly, but at least two more warriors were hit. The guide killed one more, then the Pawnees raced off across the prairie.

Several of the men leaned over in their saddles and heaved up their guts at the sight of the two bloody bodies on the ground.

Waterman laughed, but it was more from relief than joy. "Ain't purty, is it?" he asked, not expecting an answer.

"No," Tanner managed, spitting out the last of the vileness from his stomach.

"There's no more time for pukin', boys," the guide said. "We best ride and ride hard. I ain't certain of course, but there's a chance them Pawnees'll be back with some of their friends, and I ain't about to wait around for them to show up."

"The arrow?" one of the men asked, pointing.

Waterman did grin, then pulled the shaft free and dropped it on the ground. "Stuck in my medicine bundle. Barely broke the skin."

"Medicine bundle?" Tanner asked.

"Reckon it's kind of like an Indian good luck charm. Warrior usually has a vision that tells him what to put in it. Protects you from harm."

"You believe in that?" one of the other men asked skeptically.

The guide cocked an eyebrow at him and pointed to the arrow on the ground. "Now, let's ride." He galloped off, not waiting to see if the others were following.

They rode through the afternoon, the night, and most of the next day, then pulled into a clump of cottonwoods along a stream. As they were sitting around the fire, Tanner asked, "Couldn't you have given those Pawnees a little of what they asked for, Buck?"

"You questionin' me, boy?" Waterman asked harshly.

"Nope. Just tryin' to learn. Seems there was a lot of dying over something as small as a bit of powder and lead."

"Those boys weren't about to accept that or anything else. While we was negotiatin', they were sizin' things up. While they really didn't outnumber us, what they saw was a heap of greenhorns. That leader, he figured he'd kill me and takin' down the rest of you'd be no problem. Then he'd have all the supplies, all the animals, and," he paused for effect, "all the scalps."

A shiver slid up Tanner's spine, and he figured the others felt the same sensation. "Devious bastards, aren't they?"

"Most Injuns are." He grinned crookedly. "Could say the same about most white folks, too."

Tanner thought that over, then nodded. "I'd have to agree with you there."

Waterman grunted, then said, "I ain't given to handin' out compliments, but most of you boys did well against those savages. A few of you didn't do a damn thing, though. We have another encounter with

23

Injuns and it turns violent, you best do your part. Now, get some shuteye. We'll be on the trail at first light."

They had no more Indian trouble, but after another month, they began seeing dispirited men heading east. At times they had seen wagons passing them with the slogan Pike's Peak or Bust. These returning fellows, broke and broken, had crossed that out and simply written "Busted" on the canvas.

"That bad?" Tanner asked one of the men, this one on foot, trudging gloomily along.

"Yep. Maybe worse. Ain't no gold there. If there was, it's all been taken up by others. All that's left is dirt and cold water in the streams. And Indians. And bears. Don't know which of those is the worst. I suggest you turn back now before it's too late, especially before winter. You don't want to experience winter out there. Worst weather I ever saw. Cold right to your bones, snow ass-deep to a moose."

"The guidebook I got says things ain't that bad."

"Guidebook?" The man snorted. "Ain't a one of 'em worth usin' to wipe your ass with. About the only thing they're good for is helpin' start a fire."

"I'll keep that in mind. Good luck to you

back in the States."

"And good luck to you out there in those mountains. You'll need it just to survive."

"Think he's right?" asked Cal Hubbard, who had ridden up alongside Tanner while he was talking to the returner.

"About there being no gold?" Tanner shrugged. "Don't know, but I don't believe it. I reckon all these fellows going back just didn't look hard enough."

"The rest?"

"Reckon all that's true — the cold, wild animals, wilder Indians. Stands to reason weather'd be worse high in the mountains. You thinkin' of turnin' back?"

Hubbard shook his head. "Nope. Not without giving it a try for a spell, anyway."

They finally reached the creek-divided towns of Auraria and Denver City. Both places were bustling and had construction haphazardly going on all over, though the latter town seemed to be overtaking the former.

"Well, boys, I got you here, and now it's time for me to take my leave," Waterman said. "Best of luck to you all in your endeavors out there." He laughed as he rode off.

"I believe he thinks we're gonna find nothing but hard times in our search," Hubbard said.

"Trouble is, he's likely right."

"Any idea where you're plannin' to start lookin'?"

"Nope. I figure to take a day or two to rest here, then just head out there," Tanner said, waving an arm at the mountains rising in the west.

"You mind maybe partnerin' up? Might make it easier, lookin' for color and bringin' some in if we do find it."

"Aimin' to jump my claim soon's I find one, eh?" Tanner asked.

Not seeing his companion's grin, Hubbard looked aghast. "I'd never . . . I mean . . ."

"I was joshin', Cal. Sure, we can partner up. Reckon if we find any gold, there'll be enough for both of us. If we don't, well, there'll be more than enough nothing for both of us."

Tanner and Hubbard spent a couple days making sure their supplies were in order and they were rested after their long journey here, then they pulled out, having no idea of where they were going. As they got farther away from the towns, they found more canyons and streams. Many of them already had men with their pans in the water or sluices running. The two companions would nod a greeting and push on.

Winter caught up with them before too much time passed. They were ready to hightail it back to Denver City but got snowed in. When the storm ended, they decided they would ride out the winter where they were.

When spring came, they went back to prospecting but found little — just a few flecks of gold here and there. Never enough to spend more than a few days searching before moving on. But they soon found themselves in need of all kinds of supplies, so they headed down the mountain to Denver City, which had grown in the past six months. The city was abuzz with news that a number of Southern states had seceded from the United States, and war had begun between the two sides.

"What're you gonna do, Chase?" Hubbard asked.

"Go back to prospectin'."

"You ain't going back east?"

"No need to."

"But the war . . ."

"I have no stake in it, so I have no interest in taking part in it. You?"

"Ain't sure."

"I'll be leavin' for the mountains day after tomorrow. You want to join me again, be

27

ready then. If not, good fortune in whatever you aim to do."

CHAPTER 3

Chase Tanner spent two more years hunting for gold without much success. He did so alone, Cal Hubbard having headed east to join the war effort. Tanner didn't even know what side his friend had joined.

After close to three years in the mountains, Tanner had had enough. In all his roaming and prospecting, he had found barely enough gold flakes and tiny nuggets to keep him in supplies. He finally realized that placer mining was no way to get rich, and he was not willing to become a hard rock miner, something that was becoming more prominent.

So he rode into Denver, sold his mule, pick, and shovel, and took a job with Harker's freighting company. Loading and unloading wagons was not that much different from loading and unloading ships, as he had done in Pennsylvania. Seeing higher wages in driving freight wagons than loading them, he tried his hand at that. He took to it easily. That work was far better for earning a wage than searching for a pot of gold that was not there.

It was mostly a boring job, hauling freight on the roads between Denver and places like Mount Vernon or Black Hawk or any of the many other camps and towns throughout the region. Doing so during the winter on roads that were poor at best made such trips all the more adventurous. Twice, near little mining camps, he came across the bodies of men who had been killed by arrows, scalped, and mutilated. Utes were responsible, he thought. But the bigger problem was, of course, the rocky, often cliff-hugging roads.

Six months into his new job, his boss, Jabez Harker, came to him as he was loading a wagon. "How'd you like to make a bit more money, Chase?" the company's owner asked.

Tanner perked up but was wary. "Doing what?"

"Taking a wagon east to the States and back."

"By myself?" Tanner asked, ready to flatly refuse.

"No, no. Part of a train. You, Bill, and Sandy'll be driving a wagon each for me.

There'll be several others from different companies from Golden and Colorado City."

"How much more pay?"

"Regular, plus a five dollar a month bonus."

Tanner snorted in derision. "I'm supposed to take a six-month journey through Indian country for a month's extra pay? I don't think so, boss. Nope."

"Ten dollars a month extra."

"Reckon not."

"Fifteen. I got to make some profit, Chase. You should know that."

"I do, but I reckon you'll be bringing back twenty thousand, maybe thirty thousand dollars' worth of supplies that you'll sell for two or three times that."

"I can find someone else to do it."

"Then do so. Ain't too many others out here foolish enough to take on such a task." He didn't know whether that was true or not, but he played that hand anyway.

"You're a hard bargainer, Chase." Harker paused, then, "All right, double your salary."

"For every month."

"Yes. And if you do it in five months, I'll add a hundred-dollar bonus — one time, not per month."

"Two hundred, and you got a deal."

"Oh, all right. First time I've given in to an outright thief." But he was smiling.

"Hell, Mr. Harker, you'll be able to retire in luxury by next year."

Harker looked thoughtful, then smiled again. "I do hope so, Chase, but I sure doubt it."

So he headed east with ten wagons, each pulled by six mules. The trip east and back took five and a half months, what with one wagon breaking down and having to be repaired on the way by the drivers and the time it took the clerks to dicker over the prices of all manner of goods and equipment.

They encountered Indians only once, on the way back when a half-dozen Kiowas came along and asked for presents to allow them passage through their land. The men were tense and the ones being paid to guard the trains were wary, but one of the drivers from the company in Boulder had dealt with Kiowas on the Santa Fe Trail and was able to negotiate. It ended with the freighters giving the warriors two of the fifteen horses they had along, as well as some tobacco and several old, barely serviceable revolvers.

Harker was pleased enough that he gave his three drivers the two-hundred-dollar bonus even though they were two weeks past the deadline. "I hope you boys'll stay in my employ," he said as he handed out the money.

Tanner nodded, but his two fellow employees said they'd take their cash and move on to some less hazardous and hard duty.

Tanner was loading a wagon that he was about to take out on the road to some of the mining camps when the small wagon train of a competing company pulled into Denver City at the end of the trip from the States. Tanner stopped what he was doing and watched. Most of the men who had just arrived seemed agitated, scared, or both. Wondering what was going on, he stowed the box he was holding and strolled over to where the men were talking animatedly to Jeffrey McGrath, the company's owner.

"What's going on?" he asked a man who seemed to be with the group but was standing a little ways away.

"We were attacked a few days ago."

"By who?"

"Cheyennes, we think."

"Anybody hurt?"

"Two killed, both guards. Soapy Williams and Cal Hubbard."

"Cal Hubbard, you said?" Tanner demanded.

"Yep. You know him?"

"He was my partner up in the goldfields 'til a couple years ago when de decided to go off and fight in the war. Figured he was still there."

"I heard he had been wounded and got out. Didn't die then. It's too bad he died at the hands of damned savages, though."

"You boys bring his body back?"

"Hell, no, neither of 'em. Hot as it is, they'd have been mighty ripe along about now. We buried 'em as best we could after drivin' the Indians off. Didn't have the time or inclination to put markers up."

"That wasn't very decent of you."

"Hell, we were worried those damned redskins'd be back with a bunch more of their friends. You're lucky we took the half-hour to bury 'em like we did."

Tanner went back to work, wishing there was a better way to say farewell to his friend than leaving him in an unmarked grave somewhere on the prairie, but there was not. Even if he took another trip east and back, there would be no way to find the grave, and there wouldn't be much he could do if he did. He could put up a marker, but he figured that would last no more than a few days.

34

After a week, he put it out of his mind. There was nothing he could do, and there was life to be lived.

As winter curled its icy fingers around Denver City and the mountains beyond, there came a call for recruits for the 1st Colorado Cavalry. Many of the men in the unit were veterans of the Union Army's battle with the Rebels in the New Mexico Territory, but they needed more men to fill out the ranks.

While part of the cavalry's mission was to make sure the Confederates did not return to the area, it would also be assigned to protect wagons and travelers, as well as keeping the Cheyennes, Arapahos, Comanches, and Kiowas in check.

Tanner did not care for the former, but he saw the latter as a good reason to offer his services. It could be, he figured, a way to pay his respects to Cal Hubbard and pay back the Indians — any Indians, it didn't matter — who had killed his friend. He'd also get a little revenge for the attack he, Hubbard, and the others had faced on their first trip out here, as well as for the bodies of the mutilated men he had found while winding his way through the mountains on his wagon.

While he was not the best horseman and

had little experience with using pistols or rifles, he signed up and was gladly accepted. He took to the training well and was soon comfortable on a horse and with weapons. Despite his lack of experience, he was eventually promoted to corporal, much to his surprise.

During training and as the men traveled the prairie looking for Indians to kill, Tanner learned about the heroics of Colonel John Chivington. The Fighting Pastor had in large part been responsible for driving Confederate forces from the New Mexico Territory at a place called Glorieta Pass a couple of years earlier.

The tales buoyed Tanner. While that battle had not been against Indians, it showed Chivington's military talent and resolve, and those were things Tanner could respect. It also boded well for any forays against the Indians.

But month after month of riding the Plains and finding no Indians had him beginning to wonder whether he would ever get to kill any red men. To make the situation worse, another winter was nearing, and traveling was made more difficult by occasional snow, frequent brutal winds, and the constant freezing temperatures.

They finally arrived at Fort Lyon. They

were cold, tired, and sick of the poor rations they had been eating. Their rumps were sore from long days in cold hard saddles, and they were tired of traveling through the horrid weather.

By the time they reached Fort Lyon, Tanner was sure the cavalry would never fight Indians, and he took heart that his enlistment would be up in little more than a month. He would spend the rest of the winter in Denver, maybe working for Harker again. In the spring, he might just try his luck prospecting once more.

But then talk began to filter through the fort and its environs where the cavalry men were camped that Indians were nearby and an attack on them was coming soon. It's about time, he thought.

But he also heard talk that the nearby Indians were peaceful and under the protection of the Army. He didn't believe that, or maybe he didn't want to. As far as he knew, no Indians were peaceful, and the ones around here — Cheyennes and Arapahos, mostly — had been on the warpath through the Colorado Territory for several years now.

He suspected they were just lying low for the winter months, collecting annuities such as food and living comfortably. Then, when spring came, they would begin raiding again, fat and sassy after a winter of being fed well by the United States. It galled him.

So, eagerness for the imminent prospect of killing Indians overrode the tiredness, the soreness, and the cold as the troops made their way toward a place called Sand Creek on the early morning of November 29.

Anticipation grew in Tanner and the other men as they stopped and waited on a bluff overlooking the Cheyenne and Arapaho camp, quiet now in the cold darkness before dawn. Word passed around that Colonel Chivington had ordered no prisoners be taken. Tanner thought that was a little obsessive, especially with women and children in the camp, but he accepted it.

The colonel waited until dawn had fully broken and the village was just starting to come alive, then gave the order to charge.

As Tanner barreled down the slope into the camp, he was vaguely aware of an American flag on a tall flagpole outside one lodge and an old man holding a white flag. Neither really registered on him until he had shot one warrior and fired at another. He brought his carbine up to fire again and realized he was about to shoot a woman holding a little child. He jerked the weapon up and fired at the sky.

Teeth clenched, he watched the other

cavalrymen charging through the camp, killing anyone they could see, chasing fleeing women and children down the river and out onto the prairie. Small pockets of warriors made stands where they could to give their families time to escape, but they were cut down, as were the ones they were trying to protect.

"Come on, Chase, join the fun!" one of his M Company compatriots shouted as he roared past.

But Tanner would not move. He had frozen when he saw the carnage before him. It was only when some of the remaining men — the main force was running down fleeing Indians — began to mutilate bodies that he moved. But there was only so much he could do and so very much he could not. He finally rode up the bluff to where Captain Silas Soule had kept D Company out of the mêlée and asked to join that company.

CHAPTER 4

Lieutenant Eric Whittemore, the officer in charge of Tanner's original M Company, formally requested that Tanner be reassigned to his company. Captain Soule, being the ranking officer, denied the junior officer's request, suspecting Tanner faced severe punishment. As a result, an angry Whittemore filed charges to court-martial Tanner after their arrival in Denver, accusing him not only of cowardice but of desertion. As soon as he learned about it, and surprised he had not been confined, Tanner went to Soule, who had finally arrived from Fort Lyon.

"What can I do for you, Corporal?"

"You've heard about my possible court-martial?"

"No." Soule was surprised. "Tell me about it."

"Lieutenant Whittemore wants me court-martialed on claims of cowardice and desertion. He says that since I did no fightin' after the first charge and I reported to you instead of him, that I'm a coward and deserter."

"Lieutenant Whittemore has always been a horse's ass." Soule thought for a few moments, then said, "I wouldn't worry about it, Corporal." Seeing Tanner's shock, he added, "The First will be dissolved within a couple weeks at most, having fulfilled its hundred days of duty. You'll be a civilian again then, as will he unless he volunteers for service in the regular Army or another militia. Meantime, stick near Sergeant Ralston with my company."

"Yes, sir." Tanner was relieved though still wary until the official end of the volunteer cavalry's existence.

Once that happened, he went back to Jabez Harker. "I'd like to hire back on with you, Mr. Harker."

" 'Fraid I can't do that, Chase."

"Why not?" the shocked Tanner asked.

"Can't have a man like you working for me."

"What do you mean, a man like me?"

"A man who runs from his sworn duty."

"I never . . ."

"I'll have to ask you to leave my premises, Chase, or I'll have the law remove you."

Tanner started to argue but decided it would be useless. He nodded. "If that's what you want, Mr. Harker, that's the way it'll be." He left, shoulders held straight. He did not see the look of sadness in his former employer's eyes or the smirk on the face of Lieutenant Whittemore, who was standing in the corner of Harker's store.

With nothing better to do and needing time to think, Tanner headed to the Found Nugget saloon and ordered a shot of rye and a glass of beer. He tossed back the ounce of whiskey, then sipped his beer.

Suddenly Emmet Barton and Sid Landis sidled up to him at the bar, one on each side of him. "How about you buy us a drink, old pal?" Landis said, making the last word sound like an insult.

"Why don't you go to hell on an old mule?" Tanner countered.

"That ain't very friendly of you, boy," Barton said.

"Wasn't meant to be. Now go on about your business and leave me alone."

"How's it feel to be a coward, boy?" Landis asked.

"I wouldn't know. How's it feel to be a horse's ass?"

"Why, you . . ." Landis looked like he was going to try to punch Tanner, but his companion stopped him. "C'mon, Sid. He ain't someone to waste our time on, the lily-livered bastard."

Landis shook him off. "I don't take kindly to yellow-bellied scum like you hittin' me when you're too scared to join in us chastising devilish Indians."

"Worse," Barton tossed in, "you were even scared to join in fightin' the damned Rebs. You let your partner go do the fightin' while you stayed here huntin' for color. Shameful, shameful."

"Got no stake in that fight back east, and I joined up with the cavalry to fight Indians."

"Then why didn't you?"

"I signed on to fight Indian warriors, not slaughter women and kids, even if they are Cheyennes."

"There was plenty of warriors there," Barton said in a huff.

"No, there weren't. Most of the warriors from that band were off on a hunt."

"Like hell." He slapped a scalp on the bar. "That there's proof."

"That there is the scalp of a child," Tanner said flatly. "Maybe five years old, likely a girl."

Before either Baron or Landis could retort, the bartender strolled up. Looking directly at Tanner, he said, "You best leave, Mister. I don't want your kind in my place."

"Rather serve baby-killers, eh?" Tanner snapped with a look of disgust. He shook his head and left.

With nothing for him in Denver, Tanner used most of the last of the money he had saved to buy a mule, gold panning gear, and enough supplies to keep him alive for a few weeks, then headed west despite it being the dead of winter. He was lucky in that there was little snow to slow him, and he reached Central City in two and a half days. The city had grown considerably, as had neighboring Black Hawk in the year since he had been here.

Splurging, he spent the night at a hotel and had a fine supper and breakfast before heading deeper into Gregory Gulch. There were a couple of streams hidden in the forest that he and his partner Cal Hubbard had always meant to try but had never gotten around to.

He found some color in one of them. Not a great deal, but enough to keep him nearby through the winter. By the time March arrived, he had several ounces of dust and a few nuggets the size of the tip of his pinkie. It was more than enough for a short spree in a city and to buy supplies for another few months of prospecting in the mountains.

He stopped in Golden, prepared to have his spree there, but in a fit of contrariness, he decided to ride on into Denver. He stabled his horse and mule first, then got himself a hotel room. He headed to a saloon — a different one than he had visited the last time — for a couple of drinks before he paid for a bath, a haircut, a shave, new clothes, a good dinner, and an hour in a halfway-decent brothel. He was heading toward the Hog Wild Saloon when Jabez Harker stopped him. "What do you want?" Tanner asked in not very pleasant tones.

"Got a job for you," Harker said after clearing his throat. He sounded unsure of himself.

"Not interested."

"Pays well."

"I don't care, Mr. Harker. Can't see why I'd take any job you offered. Now, if you'll excuse me, there's a couple of beers waitin' for me over at the Hog Wild."

"I'll pay for 'em if you'll hear me out."

Tanner, who had started to push his way around Harker, stopped and stared at his former boss. Then he nodded, turned, and headed off, neither knowing nor caring if Harker followed.

In the saloon, Harker said, "Go take a table. I'll get the beer." Moments later, he joined Tanner at a table in an almost quiet corner of the room.

Tanner took a sip of his beer. "Tell me why I should listen to you after the way you treated me the last time I saw you."

A look of embarrassment crossed the older man's face. "Things're different now."

"Different how?"

"There was an official inquiry into the events at Sand Creek."

"So?"

"So it came out that things weren't quite what the Army leaders were telling us about events there. That there were atrocities committed."

"What's that have to do with me?"

Harker gulped down some beer, then shook his head. "Before we last met, word had gone around that you and some others had not taken part in the battle."

"More a massacre than a battle."

Harker nodded. "Anyway, word was that you and some others — mostly Captain Soule's company — had not participated and you were cowards. You were mentioned in particular."

"By who?"

"Four or five fellows. One of 'em was a

46

Lieutenant something."

"Whittemore."

"Yep, that was it."

"And you believed them?"

"I had no reason not to, considering all that was going on. All the celebrating of the Army's 'victory' over the savages."

"You should've known me better than to just accept the word of some goat-humpers calling me a coward."

"Yes, I should have. And I should've talked to you before I refused to rehire you. But, I'm ashamed to say, everyone was so glad that the Cheyennes had been whupped that anyone hiring a coward would've lost much of his business." Harker hung his head. "Sometimes business comes first, whether it should or not."

"Can't blame you for that. A man's got to look out for himself and his family. Still, would've been nice if you had talked to me before sending me packing."

"Once again, yes, I should have. I didn't, and nothing can change that. I apologize for it and hope you'll see fit to put it behind us so that we can work together again."

The hint of a smile crossed Tanner's face. "We never did work together, Mr. Harker. You were the boss, and I was your employee." He paused. "So, what's the job?"

"A trip back east and return with a wagon-load of goods, like last time."

Tanner laughed, surprising Harker. "You got some cojones, Mr. Harker. First you insult me and impugn my reputation, then a few months later, you ask me to make a trip across the country, right smack through the heart of Cheyenne and Arapaho country barely three months after a peaceful band of those Indians was massacred. No, sir. I ain't that damned foolish."

"People in Denver and many of the mining camps will be starving without a fresh supply of foodstuffs and such."

"Then let some of them make the trip."

"There's good money to be made. I'll pay you a thousand dollars for the trip."

"Heap of money," Tanner admitted. "But not enough, I reckon."

"Fifteen hundred."

"Any other wagons?"

"Three total — two of mine, one from McGrath's."

"Just us drivers?"

"No. You three, one helper for each wagon, two clerks, and ten guards."

"The guards know what they're doing?"

"All veterans."

"Veterans of what? Sand Creek?"

"I don't think so. Mustered out in Kansas

after serving a couple years in the Union Army. Came out here to look for gold, like so many others. They decided to stay in Denver for the winter before heading into the mountains to look for their fortune. McGrath found 'em and convinced them to do this. Since they've not been out here long, I'm not sure they know about Sand Creek, so they might not know how dangerous this trip could be."

"A spring trip across the prairie won't be fun, what with rain, floods, and mud."

"Probably not, but maybe the Cheyennes and Arapahos, as well as other hostiles, will be too busy on their annual spring hunt to be making war."

"Don't count on it. I heard in Golden that they raided throughout the winter. Some huntin' won't slow 'em."

"So, you'll take the job?" Harker asked expectantly.

"Reckon I am that much a damn fool. Two thousand, you said?" He grinned.

"Fifteen . . . Yes, two thousand."

CHAPTER 5

"There's a few ways we can go," the short, slender, tough-looking half-breed who had been hired to guide the caravan said. The drivers, clerks, helpers, and guards had gathered in Harker's store. "Following the Platte is too far north and goes out of the way. Takin' the Smoky Hill or the Republican are about the same. Also, the Smoky Hill goes mighty close to Sand Creek."

"Something wrong with that?" Will Walters, a former sergeant and the head of the guards, asked.

Tanner glanced at him. Deciding the veteran was simply curious, he said nothing.

"There was an attack on some Cheyennes and Arapahos there," Billy Van Eck, the guide, said. "So the Indians might be riled up down that way." He paused, then grinned crookedly. "Of course, they could be riled up anywhere between here and St. Louis.

There've been reports of raids in various places."

"We'll be watchful," Walters said.

"You ever fight Indians, Mr. Walters?" Tanner asked.

"Nope. Plenty of Rebs. No Indians bothered me and the boys on our trip out here. Only Indians I've seen were some beggars outside Leavenworth. Osage, I think somebody said they were."

"Beaten-down Osage, especially ones near the settlements, ain't Kiowas or Cheyennes."

"Well, we can hope none of 'em bothers us along the way. If they do, I reckon we'll find out just how tough they are."

Van Eck and Tanner just shook their heads.

They pulled out just after dawn two days later. Van Eck rode in front, watchful. A pair of guards rode at the head of the caravan and four others, two on each side, alongside the caravan. The last four brought up the rear.

Tanner drove the first wagon, Johnny Boyd the second, and Jim McGrath, son of the store owner, drove the third. A clerk rode alongside Tanner and McGrath, and a helper rode in the back of each wagon. Two horses were tied to the rear of each wagon.

The journey was a numbing trail of boredom until the first rainstorm, a real frog-strangler, raged over them. Hats and slickers could not hold off the pounding precipitation that slid down into shirts and puddled on wagon seats. It also turned the trail into fetlock-deep mud. Between the rain and the mud, the often-cantankerous mules became even more peevish. It also meant no fires could be made, so there could be no hot food, and worse, no coffee was available. That made the men as testy as the mules.

The rain, which had lessened for hours at a time before rushing back with a vengeance, finally stopped. The sun cautiously stuck its head out from behind the clouds, then began to proudly spread its light and warmth over the mostly barren land. The road, such as it was, turned from mud to dust within a few days.

The improved weather allowed them to hunt buffalo. There were plenty along some stretches, though Tanner thought there were not nearly as many as when he had first passed this way five or so years ago. Van Eck proved to be an excellent hunter, and the men usually were well-supplied with meat. With the cottonwoods along the streams for firewood, it made for good eating.

Three weeks in, a snowstorm swept over them. As the men huddled around a couple of fires against the cold, Bart Trotter, one of the guards, said, "If this ain't the damnedest thing I ever saw. Snow in April." He shook his head in wonder.

That too did not last more than half a day and a night before blowing itself out. The warm spring sun swiftly melted what little snow had accumulated.

Just short of three months after they left Denver, they pulled into Westport. They had had no trouble from Indians, much to everyone's relief.

The first bit of news they got when they arrived was that President Lincoln had been assassinated while they were on the trail, just a few days after the war had ended. The men were torn, being jubilant that the bloody conflict had at last ended but devastated by the murder of the President. Any celebration they might have had for the former was tempered by the sadness of the latter.

The two clerks dove straight into their work and bought supplies over a couple of weeks, sometimes from places in Westport, sometimes having someone go to St. Louis to procure larger amounts of goods.

Tanner noticed that Van Eck spent a lot of

time at one of the stores from which the clerks had purchased many supplies. Tanner stopped in one day to buy a new shirt and learned that Van Eck's father worked there. The owner was a tiny, attractive slip of a woman who was helped by her daughter, a younger and barely larger though equally attractive woman. Neither was to be taken liberties with, Tanner observed. Her husband — the girl's father — ran the saloon next door, and he was a giant of a man, as was their son.

Then they were on their way west, the wagons loaded almost to overflowing, still pulled by six mules each. Worried that the animals would be overworked, the clerks had bought an additional half-dozen mules and a few extra horses. The helpers who had been hired for the trip were tasked with herding the extra animals.

Two of the guards and one of the clerks argued for leaving Van Eck behind. "There was no trouble on the way here. Ain't likely to be any on the way back," Walters said.

"We were damned lucky to have made it here without bein' wiped out," Van Eck said. "But I'll be glad to stay here and let you boys go it alone."

"He will lead the way, Mr. Walters," Finlay Porter, the main clerk on the journey, said. Since he was in charge, his word was final.

The warriors struck near where Hell Creek entered the Republican River. Van Eck came racing toward the caravan and pulled up sharply in front of the two lead guards. Tanner moved up near them.

"Indians comin'," Van Eck said. "From the north."

"How many?" Walters asked.

"Two dozen, maybe. Cheyennes and Arapahos."

"What'll we do? Hal Thomas, another guard, asked, sounding worried.

"Make for the trees along the creek. Should give us some protection. Then you boys'll get your taste of Indian fightin'. Now ride!"

"Hold on to your hat, Mr. Porter," Tanner said as he snapped the reins to get the mules moving. The animals lumbered into motion, seemingly in no hurry. "Damn mules," Tanner muttered. "Come on, you sons a bitches," he yelled. "Move, dammit!"

The animals picked up speed. Tanner's wagon, as well as the other two, charged into the wooded strips along the creek as gunfire cracked behind them. Tanner jerked the team to a halt and set the handbrake.

"Get under the wagon, Mr. Porter."

Age hindering him a little, the clerk awkwardly hopped off the wagon and ducked under the large conveyance.

"Johnny, Jim, set the brakes! All of you get under the wagons. Hurry!" He flinched reflexively as an arrow, then another, thudded into the wagon near his head.

The extra horses and mules had swirled into the cover of the trees, where the three handlers fought to control the neighing, braying animals.

"Let 'em be, boys," Tanner yelled. "Get yourselves under cover somewhere!"

The two young men slipped off their horses and hid behind trees, then drew their pistols and began firing to little effect. Tanner had the thought that they might be more of a danger to him and the rest of the waggoners than to the Indians.

The firing had been steady even before he and the others had reached the trees. Tanner now saw several warriors go down. Others were charging through the trees but were driven back into the open, where two more went down. One of the guards fell dead, and another sank to the ground with an arrow in his side.

Tanner grabbed his rifle and fired the single-shot breech-loading Spencer twice, but all he hit was a warrior's horse. Another Cheyenne grabbed the man's arm, swung him onto his pony, and took off with the rest of the war party.

Things quieted down, and the men warily assessed the damage. Besides the dead guard and the wounded one, only one other — a young laborer who had been among those herding the extra animals — was sitting white-faced, looking at the arrow in his shoulder. Tanner knelt beside him and examined the wound. "Don't look too bad," he said. "Hurts like hell, though, I expect." When the youth nodded, Tanner gave him a small smile. "It'll hurt even more when we get it out of you."

He left the young man and went to the wounded guard. "Yours looks worse," he said, "but it likely ain't fatal."

"Looks like you didn't do much fightin'," Walters said, moving up to stand behind Tanner.

The closeness of an armed man behind his back worried the freighter, but he tried to remain calm. "That's what you were hired for," he said.

"You had helped, Buck might still be alive."

"And there's every chance he'd still be dead." Tanner rose and turned to face the veteran. "Now, are you gonna fix up these two wounded men?"

"I don't know much about doctorin'."

"I know some, so go on over there and keep watch in case those damn redskins come back. Sammy, fetch a jug of whiskey from the stores," he ordered one of the laborers.

"A celebration?" Finlay Porter asked, surprised.

"Yep. I thought it'd be nice to have a snort or two to proclaim our victory." When Porter looked apoplectic, Tanner said, "I'm joshin'. It's to knock these boys out so I can get the arrows out of 'em."

"My mother's people know about poultices," Van Eck said, "but I never learned much about 'em. Don't think we'd find much of what we needed out here anyway."

"Your mother?" Walters asked.

"I thought it was no secret that I'm a half-breed." He sounded proud of it. "My pa was a mountain man back in the '30s; Ma's Shoshoni." When Walters had trouble saying anything, Van Eck added, "You seem shocked. You shouldn't be. All Indians ain't the same, nor are all white-eyes. Shoshonis have been friendly with the whites since Lewis and Clark. Blackfeet are the biggest rapscallions other than the Comanches."

58

"But . . ."

"Your kind just finished a war, trying to kill each other to extinction. From what I gather, the two sides still hate each other and would start fightin' again should that seem like a good idea."

"That's different."

"Like hell. It's just two tribes — damn big ones, I admit, but still just two tribes — at war with each other, just like the Crows and the Sioux or the Blackfeet and, well, just about any other tribes, though disease has reduced 'em to the point where they ain't much of a threat."

"Well, maybe."

"The Cheyenne and the Arapaho used to trade with the whites. They were great friends with a man named William Bent. Little White Man, the Cheyennes called him. Married a Cheyenne, and they had four or five young 'uns together. When she died, he married her sister.

"But whites have broken treaties and kept taking Indian land, so some of the tribes fought back. There were atrocities, I must admit, but the raidin' was small considering the number of whites pouring through tribal lands. Then came Sand Creek near the end of last year."

"You were there, weren't you, Chase?"

Walters said.

Tanner nodded, wondering how Walters knew. Out of the corner of his eye, he could see Van Eck flinch and a hard look cross his face. He considered telling his side of it but decided that would be no help. He took the jug of whiskey from Sammy and bent to pour some down Doug Carter's throat.

"What about me?" Parley Quince, the wounded veteran, said.

"You're a tougher fella than this boy," Tanner said calmly. He encouraged the young laborer to keep drinking until he was about out. Then he turned to Quince.

He was sweating as much as the two wounded men by the time he finished removing the arrows and bandaging the men. Tanner looked at Van Eck. "Stay here for a spell or move on? These boys'll likely be out for a bit. We could make some room with padding to carry 'em along, or we can wait 'til morning and see if they can ride."

"Those devils might be back."

"They might wait to catch us out in the open if they're bent on revenge."

"All the more reason to move on, I reckon."

Tanner nodded and rose.

"I ain't movin' any of my goods to accommodate them," Jim McGrath said flatly.

Tanner nodded. "Johnny, Sammy, let's get to work."

"Best hurry," Walters said.

"Go to hell. You might have a couple men try to run down a few of the extra animals."

"What in hell for? Let the redskins have 'em."

Tanner almost smiled when he caught the flash of anger on Van Eck's face. "And what happens if one of your horses go lame? Or one of the mules breaks a leg?" He headed for the wagons, ignoring the guards.

The rest of the journey was mostly peaceful, but Tanner was on edge, waiting for Van Eck to confront him. The half-breed guide kept his distance, though Tanner could often feel the man's eyes on him, watching and, Tanner feared, waiting.

CHAPTER 6

As Tanner began unloading his wagon at Harker's store, the owner called him into the room at the rear he used as an office.

"You can wait 'til I finish unloading all the goods," Tanner said with a grin. He was eager for his pay, but he was also conscientious enough to feel that unloading the wagon was part of the deal.

"That's not it, Chase," Harker said hesitantly.

Tanner's back stiffened. "I'll finish the unloading. You can pay me, and I'll be on my way, Mr. Harker," he said tightly.

"What? No, no, it's not anything about you or your job."

"Then what?"

"It's Captain Soule."

"What about him? Is he all right?"

"He's dead, Chase. He was shot down just a few weeks after you left."

Tanner was shocked. It was unthinkable

that the jovial, dedicated, hard-working officer was gone. Tanner had been grateful when Soule had allowed him to join D Company that day. He was even more so when the captain had refused Whittemore's request to have Tanner returned to M Company, which would have allowed the lieutenant to punish Tanner. When Tanner had offered to testify at the inquiry into the attack to support Soule and the other officer, Lieutenant Cramer, who had refused to send his men into the fray, Soule had told him, "It's not necessary, Corporal. Only officers will do so. Besides, no reason for my men to get pulled into this mess any more than they've already been." And now the officer was gone.

"Who did it?" Tanner asked.

"Fellow named Charles Squire."

"Soon's I get done here, I'll be heading out."

"No need. He's been caught down in the New Mexico Territory. I expect they'll be bringing him back here soon." Harker's faced hardened. "If you think you'll kill him when he does, you'll have to stand in line. Any man who's ever served under Captain Soule is ready to put a bullet in that fellow. Captain Soule was well-liked by everyone. Well, everyone but Chivington and a few of his apologists," Harker added with a bite in his voice.

Tanner nodded and went back to work, doing his job woodenly. When he finished, he took the sack of gold coins Harker handed him and got himself a hotel room. He ate unenthusiastically, then bought a bottle of cheap whiskey, locked himself in his room, and drank himself into oblivion. It took more than a day to recover from the excess and a few more before he began to recover from the loss of a man he so respected.

At that point, he began wondering what he would do with his life. Denver offered plenty of opportunities, but it was the place where Soule had been killed. It was also a place where he occasionally ran into former Privates Emmett Barton, Sid Landis, and a few others, men who considered him a coward. He did not want to have to walk around feeling as if he had a target on his back all the time. He supposed he should decide soon. Winter was not far off, and if he didn't want to live in Denver, he would have to leave here soon to get to wherever he decided he would make his life.

"Mind if I sit?"

Tanner looked up at Billy Van Eck. "If

you're gonna shoot me, get it done. You don't need to pretend to be friendly to get me off my guard."

"Think I'm plannin' to shoot you?"

"I think that's a strong possibility."

"Well, I ain't plannin' to. At least, not today."

Tanner shrugged. "Suit yourself, but you can buy your own beer."

Van Eck signaled to a waiter and took the mug of beer from the tray the man held. He tossed a coin on the tray and set the mug on the table, then sat. He took a healthy drink, wiped the foam off his mouth, and asked, "So, you were at Sand Creek?"

"You know that."

"You take part?"

"What do you think?"

"I ain't sure what to think. If you were there, there's a good chance you took part, which makes you a savage son of a bitch. But if what I heard is true, you didn't take part and are considered a coward."

Tanner shrugged. "Think what you like, friend."

"Of course, there's another possibility." When the half-breed got no response, he said, "You could've been there and not taken part in the savagery, but not because you were a coward. Because you're a decent man."

"Strange thing for you to say."

"Why? Because I'm a half-breed? I'm only half-Indian because my father's a white man. All the men who ran the mountains with him were white men, and I know most of 'em. Toughest bastards you'll ever meet. Take all kinds of pain and hardship, but they would die for each other, and the others would cry over his body. They'd kill Indians by the dozen if need be and be every bit as savage as any warrior — or any of the scum at Sand Creek. But they wouldn't slaughter innocent ones. And all of 'em married Indian women."

"You should be proud of 'em." Tanner wasn't sure if he was being serious or sarcastic and didn't much care either way. "But what's all this got to do with me?"

"Be nice to know what kind of man you are."

"Why? If you find I'm a savage, you'll want to kill me. If that's the case, I'd rather you do it here and now — or try to — rather than ambushin' me."

"I ain't the kind to bushwhack someone. I wanted to kill you, I'd do it face to face."

"Good. On the other hand, if you find out I'm a coward like some people say, what

66

will you do? Shake your head in disgust and leave? That won't make your life or mine any better or different."

"There's that other possibility. I heard that a couple company commanders refused to have their men join in the barbarity. You belong to either of those units?"

Tanner hesitated. Technically he had not, at least until he had requested permission to join Captain Soule's company well into the attack. And he had killed a couple of warriors before he'd seen what kind of carnage was being wrought. He had been happy when Soule had allowed him to transfer and more so when the captain had refused Whittemore's request to have Tanner returned to M Company. And he had been devastated when he learned that Soule had shot to death a few weeks after he and the caravan had left for the States at the beginning of April.

So he didn't know how to respond to Van Eck or if he even wanted to. He sighed. "Maybe that just means those two officers were cowards too and made cowards of all their men." He paused. "This is no concern of yours, Mr. Van Eck. No matter what happened with me that day, it won't affect your life in any way."

"Reckon that's true. I just hate to see a

good man branded a coward if he ain't one."

"The guards on our travels think I am one."

Van Eck snorted. "If I was a bettin' man, I'd wager they run out on their fellow soldiers. Or at least, most of 'em."

"They fought well against those Cheyennes and Arapahos."

"Three of 'em did. The others hid behind trees and fired without lookin' like those young fellas that were along. And I saw you pulled that one wounded man out of trouble. I also saw you take a few shots — lousy shots maybe, but it looked like you were tryin' to hit some warriors — after your made sure the others were as safe as they could be."

He waited for a response but got none. "Well, reckon it's time for me to be on my way. If it means anything to you, Mr. Tanner, I don't think you're a coward. I think you're a man of principle."

Tanner held up his almost empty mug in salute. "If you're heading back east, be careful. There're a lot of Indians on the trail." He offered a wry smile.

"I'll remember that," Van Eck said with a chuckle.

Emmet Barton was not as polite as Van Eck

had been. He simply plunked himself down in the chair the guide had used only minutes ago. "So, what were you doin' talkin' to that Injun?" he asked without preliminary.

"He's only half-Indian."

"Same thing, far's I'm concerned."

"Your concerns about anything don't mean a damn thing to me, so take 'em somewhere else and leave me be."

"There's many folks in Denver, me included, who don't much like Injun lovers."

"Good to know. If I meet any, I'll let you know."

"You son of a bitch, you're one of 'em."

"What makes you say that?"

"You attacked me instead of those damned heathen Cheyennes at Sand Creek, and from what I heard, you didn't help fight off those Cheyennes that attacked your wagon train on the way here."

"I attacked you and your pals because you were gonna kill some kids and castrate an old man who was no danger to anyone. As for those who attacked our wagons, well, we had armed guards to do the fightin'."

"You know what I think?"

"Nope. Don't care, either."

Barton plunged ahead. "I think you're a coward. An Injun-lovin' yellow-belly through and through." He looked smug.

"I don't care the least little bit what you think. You are a wretched man . . . Well, more a duck fart than a man, really."

"Why, I ought to . . ."

"What you ought to do is get the hell out of my sight. I beat you once, and I can damn well do it again. And it'd be a pleasure to do so."

Barton shoved himself up so hard that the chair scraped across the floor for a ways, then fell over. He slapped his hands on the table. "You just better watch yourself, Tanner. Like I said, there's many a man around here who don't take kindly to an Injun-lovin' coward."

"And a fine day to you too, sir," Tanner said with a smirk. He watched as Barton stalked away, then took his hand off the butt of the Colt Army stuck in his belt. He wasn't an expert in its use, but he wasn't completely unfamiliar with it either. He was glad the confrontation had not required him to use it, though he was afraid it might come down to that one of these days.

Over the next week, Tanner considered his options. With the money he had received for the trip east and back, he was flush. He thought he would use some of the money to start his own business. If not in Denver, then in one of the mining towns, and there were still plenty of those up in the mountains not far from the city. The trouble with that was he had no idea of what kind of business to start. He knew no trade other than freighting, and he was reluctant to start a company to compete with Harker. Doing so elsewhere would be even tougher without knowing anyone to help. And with winter coming on, trying to get a company off the ground — especially one that was based on hauling goods — would be difficult.

A partial decision was made easier when a bullet nearly hit him in the head one night after he left a saloon and was walking back to his hotel. So that's the way it'll be, he thought. Well, reckon it's time to move on.

The next day, he went to see Harker and told him what had happened. "So, I figure I best find somewhere else to live."

"I'm putting together a small wagonload of supplies for some stores in Idaho Springs. Interested?"

Tanner thought it over. "Only if I can stay there."

"I got an old wagon you can use. Might take a little effort on your part to make sure the thing makes it to Idaho Springs, but when you get there, you can sell it if you can find anyone foolish enough to buy it. You can send the money to me with whoever is trustworthy and is making the trip here. If you can't sell it, tear it apart and use it for firewood."

"Reckon that'll do, Mr. Harker."

Chapter 7

"You don't want the whole wagon?" Tanner asked.

"Nope," the wainwright said. "Just the wheels and axles, I reckon. Nothin' else is worth it. I ain't even sure of those, but I suppose I can fix 'em if there ain't too much damage."

Tanner thought that over, then shrugged. "You take 'em off?"

"Just leave the wheels on the axles. I'll have a couple of my men haul 'em away."

Tanner looked at the empty lot where he stood next to the decrepit wagon. He had pulled in there yesterday when he arrived in Idaho Springs. He had unloaded the wagon at a store, returned to the open lot, and taken the mule and his horse to the stable, then found the wainwright. He had returned and spent the night huddled in the wagon bed. It had been cold but not unbearable.

"Reckon that'll do. I ain't hitchin' the

thing up just to move it down the street to your place if you're not buying the whole thing."

"I see no problem with that. It'd help some if you could start breakin' this old woodpile down."

"Reckon I can do that."

Money changed hands, and the wainwright left. Tanner looked at the wagon, shrugged, and then grinned. He pulled his few belongings out of the bed and set them neatly against the wall of the hardware store next to the empty lot. Then he grabbed an ax and went to work. He had made a fair amount of progress when two burly young men arrived. They joined in, and within an hour, there was a pile of wood and a pair of axles with the wheels attached. The young men hooked up both axles to a sturdy mule and pulled them down the street.

Tanner grabbed a plank and a piece of charcoal from the fire he had made the night before and hastily scribbled FIRE-WOOD. FREE. He rested the plank against the pile of wood that had recently been a small freight wagon, kicked out the fire, grabbed his belongings, and marched down the street.

He took a room at the better of the two hotels in town, then went to eat at a good restaurant. As he walked there, he was surprised by the size of the town. It had grown considerably over the past year or so. There were plenty of businesses, most still made of logs, but a few were built of planks and a couple of bricks.

After his meal, Tanner wandered to a saloon and stood in a corner, leaning against a wall, watching the patrons drinking and gambling. Since the gunshot that had barely missed him in Denver, he was wary around people. He didn't know for sure why someone had shot at him — or even if it had been aimed at him, not a stray bullet fired by some drunk — but he was determined to not let it happen again.

Two beers later, he headed to the tonsorial parlor, where he had a bath, a shave, and a haircut. He didn't have new trousers or boots, but he did have a clean shirt, which he donned. "Where's the best bagnio in town?" he asked the barber.

"Lottie's. Three doors down across the street. Brick building."

"Obliged." Minutes later, he was standing in the parlor of Lottie's bordello. He was impressed. There was a small but well-stocked bar and a quartet playing soft music, plus couches scattered around. Some were occupied by couples, others by attractive, well-dressed young women.

"What can I do for you?" asked a plump middle-aged woman with an unpainted face. She was wearing an expensive dress and even more expensive jewelry.

"Well, I'd like five pounds of flour, a frying pan, and . . ."

The woman looked at him as if he were insane.

Tanner gave the madam a charming smile. "There ain't but one reason a man would come here, ma'am."

"Reckon so," Lottie said, unaffected by his charm. She looked him up and down, appraising him. "My prices aren't cheap, and I only allow a select kind of man in here."

"And you don't think I'm such a man." It was a statement, not a question.

"You are correct."

"How much are your usurious rates?"

"I don't like your attitude, mister."

"And I don't like yours. I can pay what you ask unless you're asking way above what I see as the offerings. Don't go judging a man just 'cause he ain't wearing some fancy outfit."

"I'm a good judge of men."

"Not in this case."

Angry, she waved a hand at a good-size

76

man who had been leaning against a wall at the back of the room.

"Bouncer?"

"Yes. He will escort you from the premises."

"And if I don't want to leave?"

"He will make you, and it will be painful for you."

Tanner smiled. "He tries to lay a hand on me, I will pound him into a puddle on the floor."

"Cocky, aren't you? Clem there is not one to mess with."

"Neither am I when pushed."

"Let's go, mister," Clem said firmly, grabbing Tanner's left arm.

Tanner, strengthened by years of moving large crates and barrels and used to fighting a team of mules pulling a large wagon, swung his right fist. It caught Clem on the side of the face, cracking his jawbone and, Tanner figured, his eye socket.

Clem went down in a heap, eyes rolling up.

"You need better help, ma'am."

"I reckon I do," Lottie said, voice shaking. "Well, I think we can accommodate you. Why don't you have a drink, then choose which of my fine gals you'd like to spend the evening with."

"All these gals look quite lovely, and I reckon I might enjoy spending a heap of time with any of 'em. But considering that the boss is a nasty, unthoughtful old harridan, I expect I'll go somewhere else."

"There's no other place in Idaho Springs like mine," the madam said. She watched in horror as more than half the men who had been talking with the parlor girls suddenly had business elsewhere and headed for the door.

"Don't matter. Nearabout any place'd be better than here."

Lottie nodded her head at the door. "I've lost a good amount of money because of you, mister.

"Those men'll be back."

"I suppose they will, but they may cause trouble."

"Why's that?"

"With Clem out of commission, they might take liberties, knowing they'll not be run out of here."

"Like I said, you need better help."

Lottie's eyes widened as an idea struck her. "Why don't you take the job? You've shown you can handle yourself. Those men will know better than to mess with you."

Tanner thought that over.

"Fifteen dollars a week, six days, nine

78

hours a day. Plus, you can have any of my girls you want as long as it's not during business hours."

"Sounds tempting, but it means I'd be working for you, and that doesn't sit well with me."

"I know I've been unfriendly so far, but I can be a pleasant boss."

Out of the corner of his eye, Tanner saw several of the women flinch. "Reckon I'll have to turn you down, ma'am."

Lottie was about to argue, but the look on Tanner's face told her it would do no good. "Well, I am sorry to hear that. The offer still stands if you change your mind."

"Nice to know. Good evening, ma'am." Annoyed, Tanner left.

On the advice of a bartender, Tanner wandered over to Lil's Place. The girls were not quite as pretty, the liquor was not as high class, the music was provided by a solo piano player, and the furnishings were not as refined. While Lil was not friendly, she wasn't unpleasant either.

After a fine time at Lil's, Tanner went back to his room and fell on the bed, tired. In the morning, he had a nice meal and then wandered around town, thinking. He had been here only for two days, and he was already bored. He needed something to do.

He even considered going back to Lottie's and taking her up on her offer, but he discarded that notion. He knew he could never work for that woman.

A week later, he took on the job of carrying mail and small amounts of supplies from Idaho Springs to other mining towns in the area: Black Hawk, Central City, Empire, and Georgetown. It was an easy job for him if you didn't count driving a small cart or wagon through snow-choked passes or valleys and up and down steep rocky slopes.

He generally enjoyed the work, appreciating the solitude. He had taken the job in part because he had decided that being around people for too long was troublesome. He bundled up in a bearskin coat, a bearskin hat, and bearskin gloves, then climbed into the cart or wagon seat, happily slapped the reins on the mule's rump, and off he went.

It was for the most part a boring job, driving mile after mile on snow-covered trails that passed as roads until he pulled into a town, deposited the mail at whatever passed for a post office, picked up more, and drove on to the next town. The most excitement he had was a good meal at one of the restaurants in Georgetown.

That is, until he was stopped by two

masked men sporting revolvers in their hands. "Stop right there, pard," one said. "Toss down the strongbox, and we'll be on our way."

"What strongbox?" Tanner was confused.

"Don't fool with us, boy."

"I ain't foolin' with you. I'm not carryin' a strongbox."

"What are you carryin'?"

"Mail, mostly."

"Mail? What kind of mail?"

"Letters and such from people back east."

"Might be worth something, Hal," the second man said. "Banknotes or something."

"Let's see them letters," Hal said.

"They're in the back. Canvas sack. I doubt you'll find anything of value."

"Why not?"

"You think people back east will be sending anything valuable to men out here in the middle of the mountains looking for gold?"

"Maybe not. Go look, Chaz."

"Hey, Hal, there's a bunch of other stuff back here."

"What kind of stuff?"

"Flour, some nails, a few other small things for the mercantile in Central City. Some candy too if you have a sweet tooth."

Tanner almost smirked. He did not feel very threatened by these two fools. There was a chance that they might get angry about not finding treasure and shoot him just for the sake of doing so, but he didn't think that likely.

Chaz pulled out the small canvas sack of mail, opened it, and dumped the contents on the frozen ground. He tore open a few envelopes and pulled out the papers, then looked them over, growing more agitated by the moment. "Ain't nothin' here but letters, Hal."

"Told you, boys," Tanner said with a shrug. As the two would-be robbers stood there trying to think of what to do, Tanner added, "What you boys're looking for is a bigger wagon heading east from these places. They'll be bringing gold to Denver."

"And maybe back, too," Hal said.

"Could be, but it'd be in a larger wagon than this."

"Bah. Let's go, Chaz."

Tanner considered telling the two to find another line of work, but he thought that might be too much for them and they'd start shooting. He settled for climbing down, picking up the letters, putting them back in the sack, and tossing that in the back of the wagon. Then he was on his way again.

He didn't give too much thought to the attempted robbery until he was back in Idaho Springs. Then he decided it would be wise to protect himself. He thought he should be better prepared in case more accomplished robbers stopped him. He carried his Colt with him, but it had been stuck in a coat pocket, and he would've had a devil of a time getting it out if he had needed to. He wasn't sure how well he could shoot with it anyway. He had never been that good with a revolver, and he had not used his in quite some time.

So he made the trip to Denver, where he had a gunsmith make sure his six-gun was in good working order. He bought a good supply of powder, lead, and percussion caps and returned to Idaho Springs. On days when he was not on the road, he was in a small branch of the gulch practicing firing his pistol. He also cut the flap off his old Army holster and began wearing it on his left hip, butt forward. He left his coat open a little, not enough to let in the cold but enough that he could reach the revolver without much resistance. He felt better about his trips then, though he realized that if men were intent on robbery, he wouldn't stand a chance.

CHAPTER 8

Tanner found Idaho Springs to be a pleasant place once spring arrived, and he decided to stay for a while. He continued his mail runs, a bit more wary with the arrival of warmer weather. Not too many would-be robbers risked waiting out in the snow and cold in the hope that a wagon with worthwhile loot would come along. With the advent of spring, there was a greater chance they would be out and about.

While Tanner thought there was a good possibility of that happening, he did not expect to be stopped by his old "friends" Hal and Chaz. He pulled the wagon to a halt and casually rested his hand on the grip of his revolver. "Never thought I'd see you boys again."

"We're just out here takin' care of business."

"No, you aren't. If you were, you wouldn't have stopped me again. You know I ain't carrying anything of value."

"Didn't know it was you."

"Well, now that you do, let me by and go your own way."

The two would-be robbers holstered their pistols and waved Tanner forward. As he drew up alongside the two, he stopped again. "You know, boys, if you're gonna rob folks and hope to get away with it, I suggest you not use your names with each other." He grinned and snapped the reins as he moved off, unafraid that they would do anything. If they were as poor shots as they were robbers, he was safe.

Tanner picked up the small sack of mail at the Idaho Springs post office. As he turned to leave, he bumped into as fine-looking a woman as he had ever seen.

"Pardon me, ma'am," he said, stumbling over his tongue a little.

"No apology needed. It was my fault."

Gathering his nerve, he grinned. "Well, I reckon that must be true."

The woman looked at him in shock.

"I expect you were distracted. If you weren't, you would've seen this big ugly galoot and got your pretty self out of the way before the clumsy oaf almost knocked you down."

She thought that over a moment, then she too grinned. "Well, certainly big, but almost handsome." She blushed.

"Well, thank you, ma'am. Now, I best be moving on." He tipped his hat and left. As he climbed onto his wagon to head out, he looked back. He couldn't see her. Not in person, but he had a good view of her in his mind. It was quite a pleasing picture, and it presented some intriguing possibilities in his mind, even if they were unlikely to go anywhere.

Two weeks later, when he returned to Idaho Springs, he spotted the woman on the street. He took a deep breath, then approached her. "Pardon me, ma'am."

She looked at him, startled. "Do I know you, sir?"

"Well, not exactly." He took off his hat. "I'm the fella who bumped into you at the post office a couple weeks ago."

She smiled. "Ah, yes. 'The big galoot,' as I believe you referred to yourself."

"Yes, ma'am." He grinned ruefully. "Name's Chase Tanner, and I'd like to apologize for joshin' you about it."

"No need, Mr. Tanner. There was no harm done in the slight bump and nothing amiss in your little joke."

"Thank you . . ." He cocked his head in

87

question.

She hesitated for a moment, then said, "Lisbeth Spicer."

"Lisbeth." He rolled it around on his tongue, then nodded. "A pretty name befittin' such a pretty woman. Are you related to Steve Spicer who owns the hardware store?"

"He's my father."

"A fine man." He paused. "I have to ask, ma'am. Is it Miss or Mrs. Spicer?"

"That is no concern of yours, Mr. Tanner," she said tightly.

"I apologize. I just thought that if it was 'miss," you might consent to allowin' me to court you. Of course, if you're not married, I expect you have to drive away beaus with a whip."

"Well, I do have several callers," she said with a laugh, "but perhaps another will be all right, at least if my father permits it. Please stop by my father's house this evening. A white plank house near the corner of Colorado and 14th Street."

"I will do so. Thank you."

Steve Spicer knew Tanner and liked him even though he had heard rumors about the young man's lack of courage. He didn't think the rumors were true, but one could not be sure. "Have you fought Indians, Mr.

Tanner?" he asked.

Tanner's back stiffened. "I have."

"What kind?"

"Red ones."

"Where and when?"

"Here and there, sometime in the past." He rose. "I'm sorry I wasted your time, Mr. Spicer. Please tell Miss Lisbeth I won't bother her again."

"Why not?" Lisbeth asked as she entered the room.

"A misunderstanding, my dear," her father said hastily. "I was about to clear things up and tell Mr. Tanner that he has my blessing to come calling on you — if your mother does not object."

"She doesn't," Lisbeth said and grinned. "I asked her before I asked you."

"She's a hardheaded girl, Mr. Tanner."

"Best kind." He grinned too. "Maybe."

"So, will you escort me to the milliner's, Mr. Tanner?"

"Be happy to, long as I don't have to go inside."

"Might be a long wait."

"It'll be worth it." He smiled as she blushed.

Lisbeth put on her bonnet, wrapped a shawl around her shoulders, and headed out. Tanner followed in the billowing wake of her skirt.

Tanner escorted Lisbeth around town as often as he could when he was there and found himself smitten with the tall, slender young woman. He thought, or maybe hoped, she was beginning to favor him over her other suitors.

"Good evening, Miz Spicer," former Lieutenant Eric Whittemore said as he stopped at the table shared by Lisbeth and Tanner in Belaw's restaurant. He was flanked by Emmett Barton and Sid Landis.

"Good evening to you, Mr. Whittemore."

"Is this man a new caller of yours?"

"I think that is none of your concern," Lisbeth said, irritated.

"Perhaps not, ma'am, but I do believe your father would be most disappointed if he was to know that one of your callers is a coward."

"I don't believe that."

"It's true, sadly. Instead of chastising the Cheyennes at Sand Creek a year and a half ago, he chose to try to prevent my men from doing so. I led one of the companies during the attack."

"If that is the truth, why has he not been punished?"

"I planned to have him court-martialed,

but two obstacles arose: he took refuge with another company, one whose commander did not allow his men to fight, and before I could bring Mr. Tanner here back under my command, the militia was disbanded after the terms of its enlistment ran out."

"Well, thank you for that information, Mr. Whittemore. I will certainly talk with Mr. Tanner about it. In private, not out here in public."

Whittemore looked disappointed but smiled. "Of course." He touched the brim of his hat and walked away, followed by his minions.

The rest of their dinner was eaten in an uncomfortable silence and was soon over. Tanner and Lisbeth left and strolled down the street to the Spicer house, where they stopped outside.

"So, is it true?" Lisbeth asked

"Is what true?"

"Are you a coward?"

"If it were true, would I admit it? If I denied it, would you believe me?"

"Did you do what Mr. Whittemore said?"

"If you look at it through his eyes, yes."

"And your eyes?"

"Killin' women and babies is not a battle."

"There were no women and children killed there."

"Yes, there were. Many of them."

"Well, maybe a few were there, but it doesn't matter. They are savages, worthy of our anger and retribution."

"So, killin' women and babies is all right?"

"They have killed women and children throughout the territory and done hideous things to the bodies. They deserve to be punished as severely as is possible."

"What those men did at Sand Creek drove them down to the level of the savages, as the Indians are — rightfully in many cases — called."

"Sometimes men must do things that are not what civilized men would normally do. It is unfortunate but necessary at times."

"I am surprised that such a genteel woman would have such bloodthirsty thoughts."

"As I said, sometimes men are called on to do things they do not favor to pay savages back in kind so they learn the error of their ways."

"I see. Do you know of the military's investigation into the matter?"

"Yes. And the results were a pack of lies used to malign our courageous soldiers."

"They were more savage than any Indians I ever heard about." Tanner sighed. "Well, I reckon there's no use discussin' it anymore. I enjoyed the little time we had together,

Lisbeth, and I wish you well. I hope you find a suitable husband."

He walked away, more irritated that she was one of the many people here who discounted the evidence and the military's investigation than by losing any relationship with her. He was also angry that Whittemore and others were still telling people he was a coward a year and a half after the events at Sand Creek. Worse, some people still believed the lies.

He could understand people here hating Indians after the attacks warriors had made on ranches and other outlying places. However, he could not understand them countenancing atrocities, which was what they were doing by ignoring the findings of the military's investigation. It also puzzled him that Whittemore, Barton, and the others were still hounding him after all this time. It made no sense to him. Things were over and done, or should be.

He was in a poor frame of mind when he began his next run to the other towns two days later. He found a way to vent some of his anger when another would-be armed robber popped up from behind a boulder.

He pulled the wagon to a halt and slid his hand to the grip of his Colt. "What do you want?" he asked harshly.

"What do you think, you fool? Hand over whatever valuables you got."

"Only thing of value I got is this," Tanner said, pulling his revolver and firing twice. The man was so startled that he did not fire his own weapon before he went down with two slugs in his chest.

Tanner climbed down from the small wagon and found the man's horse. He brought it to the wagon, tossed the body over the saddle, and tied it down, then hitched the reins to the back. He rode on. In Central City, he handed the body over to Abe Culver, head of the vigilance committee. That was the closest thing the place had to a law enforcement agency.

"You have to kill him?" the man asked.

"Nope. I could've let him rob me and maybe shoot me. I wasn't in the mood to allow that. Besides, you would've hanged him if you'd caught him."

Culver grinned. "So true, Mr. Tanner. I'll see to the body and send you the bill."

"You can send it as you like. I ain't payin' it."

Culver looked at him in surprise. "You killed him. You'll foot the bill for his burial."

"Like hell, I will. You don't like that, I'll just turn around and take him back where I shot him and leave him there. Or you can

94

pay some fella a dollar to dig a hole just outside of town and dump him in it. Don't matter to me either way."

Culver stared at him for a few moments, then nodded. "City'll pay for it. Or not. If the latter, he'll get a shallow grave out behind Burkhead's outhouse."

Tanner untied the horse from the wagon and handed the reins to Culver. "I believe I have some mail for you, Abe."

"Hope it's good news for a change."

"That's a hope for all of us."

CHAPTER 9

Tanner was sitting at a table in the shadows near the rear of the Silver Bucket, watching the saloon's patrons with disinterest. He had arrived in Denver the day before to pick up a new load of supplies for various stores in the mining towns and was taking a break before heading back to Idaho Springs. His disinterest changed when Baxter, one of the men he'd hit at Sand Creek and whose first name he had never gotten, walked in. He tensed, expecting trouble, but he waited, biding his time.

Baxter ordered a whiskey but turned down the cigar the bartender offered. In the mirror behind the bar, Tanner saw the man smile. "Rather have a cigarette," Baxter said. He pulled out a cigarette paper, then his tobacco pouch. He grinned again, holding out the sack. "Like it?"

The bartender laughed. Is that . . ."

"Yep, memento. Came from a Cheyenne,

96

I think she was. Maybe Arapaho. Don't matter. As you can see, she was well-rounded. Her tit turned into a right fine and sizable tobacco pouch, wouldn't you say?"

"Indeed it is. Be kind of nice to have one," the bartender said before walking away to wait on another customer, still smiling.

Seething, Tanner kept an eye on Baxter. He was tempted to confront the man but decided this was not the time or the place. After an hour, Baxter left. Tanner did too a few minutes later. Once outside, he followed the former soldier. As the thick-bodied veteran stepped off the sidewalk, Tanner sidled up beside him and smashed an elbow and a forearm into the man's face. Baxter stumbled into the alley, and Tanner hit him again.

Baxter slumped against the wood wall of the bakery. "What the hell?"

"Where'd you get the tobacco pouch?" Tanner demanded though he knew.

"Sand Creek." He grinned. "Wasn't the only souvenir I took," he said proudly. He jiggled the necklace of ears and fingers. "I had everything tanned soon's I got back here. Been carryin' one and wearin' the other ever since. Got me some good rings and earrings too, worth a fair amount of cash."

"Think you're a real hero, don't you?"

"Yeah. What's it matter to you?" He stopped and stared. "Hey, you're that cowardly, Injun-lovin' son of a bitch who . . ."

"Yep. And you're one of those baby-killin' sons a bitches who were there."

"I didn't get any of these off no babies." He sneered. "And if you had any stones, you'd have some nice decorations like me."

"Doesn't take stones for a man to kill women and kids and then hack them up. You may think I'm afraid of killin' Injuns, but I ain't. Even if I was, doesn't mean I'm against killin' a chicken-hearted, baby-killin' white man."

He slammed Baxter in the face again, then began pounding him. After a few minutes, he was breathing heavily, and Baxter was moaning on the ground. Kneeling on top of him, Tanner said, "Since you have an Indian-tit tobacco pouch, maybe I'd like to have me a white man's nut sack tobacco pouch." Then he leaned back. "Nah, yours wouldn't hold enough for even one smoke." He pulled the pouch and necklace off the man's neck and started to walk away. He heard Baxter struggling to rise and turned slowly to see him reaching for his revolver. "Don't," he warned.

"To hell with you." The veteran continued to pull his six-gun.

With a sigh at the necessity, Tanner pulled his Colt and shot him. Then he hurried down the alley away from the main street in case someone came to investigate. Half an hour later, he buried the grisly "souvenirs" in the bank of Cherry Creek, hoping that might bring some solace in the afterlife to the people from whom they had been taken.

"What the hell happened to you, Chase?" Jabez Harker asked, eyes widening at the sight of Tanner.

"Several fellas decided to do a war dance on me." Tanner's face was a mottled masked of various hues. One eye was mostly swollen shut, and his lips were puffy. Two broken ribs were wrapped tightly in bandages, and he had a splint on his left forearm.

"Why?"

"Didn't like that I killed a pal of theirs a few days ago. Don't know how they figured it was my doin'. The bastard was carrying a couple of sick mementos of Sand Creek — part of a woman's body as well as a necklace of fingers and ears. He said he had also taken some jewelry. I reckon he cut off the fingers and ears to get at it."

"That's horrible. Still, while I hate to say

it, Chase, many folks around here aren't bothered by such things, even after all this time."

"I know. Still don't set right with me."

"Get used to it, I'd say. More and more people are feeling that way again, like they did before that happened. Just like before, Indians are running wild across the Plains. Most raids are farther east in Kansas, but some are still raiding here in the territory. Mostly along the Smoky Hill Trail and the Republican River, though elsewhere too. The attacks are even worse than before, some say. Many are angry the Army hasn't been able to run the Indians down and put an end to the killing and raiding."

"Retaliation for Sand Creek."

"True, but that doesn't make it any better. Trails are more dangerous than ever, which makes getting supplies from back east more hazardous and expensive."

"Reckon it does. There won't be an end to it 'til the Indians are penned up on reservations, and that might take some time."

"Why do you say that?"

"Never-ending circle of violence. Whites have been running across Indian territory for a long time, killin' or drivin' off the buffalo, stakin' claims to or seekin' gold on

Indian land. Traders cheatin' 'em at every turn. The Indians fought back, then the whites sought revenge. Then the Indians retaliated. And so it keeps going."

"Does seem endless."

"Maybe not endless, but it certainly won't end soon. The Indians aren't about to give up their way of life, and white men aren't about to quit taking Indian land."

"So, what're you going to do?" Harker asked after a long pause.

"Recover first. Then, I ain't sure. I'm not much given to running. Maybe go back to the gold fields outside Idaho Springs. Keep away from towns for a spell and try my luck again."

"You won't get rich that way."

"That's a fact, but it should keep me away from people most of the time. Besides, I still have most of the money you paid me for that run back east."

"You might still be hounded if those men want to keep dogging you. And they might go further than they did with this beating."

"They might just find more than they bargained for."

"You going to kill them?" Harker asked, shocked.

"Not in cold blood, no. But if they come at me, I'll not hesitate to." Tanner sighed.

"Tell the truth, I wish they'd just leave me alone, but I don't reckon that's gonna happen. It doesn't make sense, though, to keep hounding me so long after that happened."

"No, it doesn't. Well, take care of yourself, and recover first. There's a job here anytime you want one."

"Thanks, Mr. Harker."

Tanner spotted Jabez Harker coming out of the barber shop and stopped, waiting for him to cross the street.

"Been looking you, Chase," the store owner said. "You're looking much better."

"Feeling much better. Everything is mostly healed up."

"Good. Very good. Glad to hear it."

"So, why have you been looking for me?"

"Have you decided on what you'll be doing, Chase?"

"Not really. Frank Belmont over in Idaho Springs is after me to take up the mail deliveries again, but I'm not taken with the idea of doing that. Too uncomfortable for me there these days." Harker looked at him in question, but he said nothing further.

"You have any objection to driving wagons and hauling supplies?"

"Can't say as I do. Why?"

"Might have a proposition for you. I'm

opening a store in a town called Kiowa a few days' ride or so southeast of here. If I can, I'll have a wagon diverted on the trail from Missouri there directly. But with the Indian raids and all, it might be easier to have 'em all delivered here."

"I ain't haulin' wagons between here and Missouri. Two trips were enough."

"I don't expect that, no," the store owner said. "What I'm figuring is that, like I said, most of the goods will be coming to the store here in Denver. What I need is someone to haul what's needed from here to my new place in Kiowa. Beyond that," Harker added hesitantly, "I'll want deliveries made to the places out on the prairie. The ranchers and farmers out that way can't often get to town for supplies, so I'm planning to supply them from the place down there."

"If I remember correctly, the Cheyennes and Arapaho are still raidin' out there."

"True. That's part of the reason they can't get to either Kiowa or here. They're afraid of leaving their places long enough to make the trip."

"So, you want me to brave warlike heathen Indians so those folks can stay comfortably forted up in their homes?" Tanner asked dryly.

"Something like that. But none of the

places you'll be visiting are all that far out on the prairie. The Indians haven't raided near any of those places. Too close to Denver."

"Then why are they all stickin' close to home?"

"You know the people in the territory. One Indian raid a hundred miles from anyplace becomes all the Indians on the Plains, rampaging everywhere."

"Sounds like how we got to Sand Creek, which brings up another problem about me doing this."

"What's that?"

"What's gonna happen when these good folks learn I'm an Indian-lovin' coward?"

"Hadn't thought of that since I don't believe that. What makes you think they'll think that?"

"Whittemore and his minions are making sure people keep having that impression, as we talked about not so very long ago."

"And you think those ill-natured rumors will follow you to Kiowa and out onto the prairie?"

"Don't you?"

"Well . . ."

"They will, though for the life of me, I don't know why. I don't give a damn about Whittemore and the rest trying to sully my name in Kiowa so much, but it could be bad for your business if those farmers and ranchers hear the rumors and start believing 'em. Especially half-panicked as they are."

"To hell with them," Harker said with a huff.

Tanner shook his head. "That's no way to run a business and you know it, Mr. Harker."

"Yes, I know," the store owner said. "I can't believe even a zealot like Whittemore will be riding all over the prairie, especially with the fear of Indians raiding, just to tarnish your good name. In Kiowa, yes, but among the farmers and ranchers? I don't think so, particularly since, as I said, those folks won't be going to Kiowa or Denver very often, if at all."

"Let me think on it, Mr. Harker."

Three days later, Tanner walked into Harker's store.

"Well?" the owner asked.

Tanner laughed. "A little anxious there, aren't you?"

Harker sighed. "Sorry, Chase. Trying to get things set up in Kiowa as well as keeping things running here has made me a bit grumpy."

"It's all right."

"So, have you decided?" Harker asked, trying to keep the eagerness out of his voice.

"Reckon I'll be a fool once again and take the job. I don't know how you do it, Mr. Harker, but you keep talking me into doing crazy things like this. What's really strange about it is I have plenty of money left from that run back east. I could easily head to the States or even go elsewhere and live comfortably, at least for some time. But no, I let you talk me into taking an ill-advised job."

"For which I am thankful."

"You know of a good cabin-builder?"

"I think so. Why?"

"I'm gonna take a run down there and find a spot for a cabin. I don't intend to live in town, so I'll need a decent place to hang my hat."

"I'll find someone." He smiled. "And I'll pay for it."

"Obliged, Mr. Harker."

CHAPTER 10

The cabin two miles from Kiowa was no mansion, but it was comfortable enough for Tanner. It was one room with a small cast-iron stove and a kitchen area on one side, a table with four chairs in the middle, and a bed along the right wall. There were windows with glass in the left wall, the rear wall, and the front wall to the right side of the door. A cottonwood-lined stream ran near the back of the cabin, and a barn stood near the left wall. The barn was large enough for a few horses or mules as well as the small, sturdy wagon Tanner would be using.

"What do you think of the cabin?" Harker asked when Tanner walked into the new store in Kiowa. The place was a jumble of crates and barrels and stacks of goods, everything from hammers and nails to dresses and bonnets.

"It'll do just fine. Could use a couple more blankets, though."

"There's some over there," Harker said, waving his arm vaguely toward a corner. "Take what you need."

"Will do when I get back." Tanner went outside, enjoying the summer's warmth and the light breeze that seemed to be a constant out here. He wandered around the town, which was small and unformed yet. Harker's store was the biggest building, but there were other businesses: a blacksmith shop, a livery stable, three saloons, one building that Tanner guessed was a brothel, a ramshackle eatery, and a small stage station, as well as several family homes.

When Tanner returned to the store to grab a couple of blankets, Harker said, "Come on back tomorrow, Chase. We'll figure out a route for delivering supplies to the various ranches."

"I don't know why you built me that cabin," Tanner said after Jabez Harker had shown his employee where he had to deliver supplies. "These farms and little ranches are like horse manure — all over the place. I'll never be able to use that damn cabin."

"It's not that bad."

"Yes, it is. The closest place is eight, ten miles from here. The rest are spread out over miles from there. Likely take me more than a week to make a circuit of those places, and I ain't sleepin' out on the prairie."

"You can stay at whatever place you're at when dusk comes. I explained that to the people. You're to be fed and housed when you arrive near dark. They'll also make sure your animals are cared for. I suggest you go a different way each time, so you don't end up staying at the same places every time. Besides, it's not like you'll be out there all the time, Chase. There'll be a week or more between those trips."

"And Denver?"

"Once every month or month and a half."

"You sure of all this?"

"Yes. If any of those folks renege on their promise to accommodate you, let me know. They'll change their tune when they either have to come here or to Denver or do without supplies."

"Reckon I'll believe you. For now. When do I make my first trip?"

"Next week."

"Just wondering, boss. How do we know what these people will want?"

"Sometimes, one of the younger men or older boys will make the rounds of the places, then come here with orders. Sometimes, they've said they'll let you know what they'll want for next time. A few near the stage route will stop the driver and give him a letter to bring here. And Mort will make sure you have extra of commonly used goods just in case."

"And how do you get paid for all these supplies?"

Harker smiled. "Ah, that's the other thing I meant to mention. You'll collect the money when you deliver the goods."

"You're joshin' me, Mr. Harker, right?"

"Well, no."

"When were you planning on telling me this if I hadn't asked just now?"

"Just before you left."

It was the thing that had bothered Tanner most about taking this job, and he came close to reneging on his acceptance. "I don't like it, Mr. Harker."

"I can understand that. But I trust you, Chase, I trust you. You've worked for me a long time and have never given me a reason to doubt your honesty."

"It ain't me I'm worried about. Some wanderin' miscreants know I'm ridin' around with pockets full of your money, they might think to relieve me of that cash. Of course, it ain't my money, so no great loss to me," he added with a grin. "But those fellas might think to do me harm to get it."

"You'll be fine, Chase."

Tanner still didn't like it, but he finally acquiesced.

"Now, if you'll excuse me, I have a lot to do to get all these goods sorted out."

Tanner pulled out of Kiowa five days later, his wagon loaded with all kinds of goods. It was a fair-sized wagon, so he had two mules pulling it. His riding horse was tied to the rear of the conveyance.

The people in the first two places, one a smalltime ranch with two families crowded into one large cabin and the other a farm with three families stuffed into two cabins, were open and friendly. They were happy to have the foodstuffs, hardware, and tools Tanner had brought. The third, another small ranch with a single family living in a soddie, which Tanner reached just before dark, did not seem happy to see the waggoner. Just before arriving, he spotted a rider trotting away from the house. There was something familiar about the man, but Tanner couldn't place it. He shrugged. He wondered why someone would be leaving the house so close to dark, and he also wondered about it when he received an inhospitable greeting from the homeowner.

Supper was a strained affair, with the patriarch and matriarch being quite stand-offish. It annoyed Tanner, especially as he could not determine why the family was acting the way it was.

"You'll have to sleep in the barn, Mr. Tanner," Fritz Haffner said after the meal. "There's hay. No oats or corn, though."

"That'll do."

"I expect you to be on your way at first light." There was no friendliness in the man's voice.

"I do something to upset you, Mr. Haffner?" Tanner's tone was harsh.

"Nein, nein. Why would you ask such a t'ing?"

"You ain't being exactly hospitable, but maybe that's just your way." Tanner put no stock in the thought, but it let the homeowner believe it if he wished, yet kept the peace.

After unhitching the wagon and seeing to his three animals — the meal had been ready just after Tanner had unloaded Haffner's supplies, so he'd put off the tasks — Tanner was standing just outside the barn, enjoying the star-speckled sky. He wondered about the lack of hospitality here but came up with no solution. He shrugged and went to sleep.

After an uncomfortable morning meal, Tanner hitched the mules to the wagon, tied the horse to the back, and rode off. He looked back once and saw Haffner watching him. It irked him, and he began to wonder if the man he had seen riding away yesterday was somehow connected to the surliness.

As he drove along, it occurred to him that the reason he'd thought something was familiar about the man was that it was Emmet Barton. "Son of a . . ." he whispered. If it really was Barton, that could be the reason Haffner had been so surly.

Thinking Barton was heading toward the next place Tanner had been planning to visit, he decided to skip it and head to another instead. It was a small ranch run by a half-breed named Charlie Wilkins and his Osage wife, Nettie. He and Wilkins and the man's two older sons, both in their twenties, unloaded his batch of supplies, then sat down to an early supper.

While they were eating, Wilkins said, "You look troubled, Mr. Tanner."

Tanner considered what if anything to say, then nodded. "You have a visitor today?"

"Nobody but you. Why?"

"You ever heard anything about me?"

"Can't say as I have. Why?"

113

"I was at Sand Creek." He almost smiled as Wilkins stiffened. "I didn't take part. In fact, I tried to stop some of the others from their atrocities. Because of it, some men who did take part are passing around rumors that I'm a coward and an Indian lover." He did smile this time. "One of 'em was at another place — Fritz Haffner's — I stopped at yesterday. I was treated like a rabid wolf by the people. I figured Barton was headin' to the next place I was gonna visit, so I skipped it and came here first."

"If this fella knows who I am, he'll not be stoppin' by here. Not at a place with a half-breed and an Osage woman."

"If he just knows the name, he might not realize who you are."

"True. So, what do you intend to do?"

"Ain't sure."

"It's still early, but why not stay here for the night? If he does show up, you and I can talk to him."

"I don't think he'll like that."

"No, he won't."

"But I don't want to get you in any trouble. He shows up here and we confront him, he'll likely go back to Kiowa and maybe Denver as well as to all the ranchers and farmers here to let them know there's two Indians — six if you count all your kids

— living in their midst."

Wilkins laughed. "No Indians here. Just a smalltime rancher and his family. Granted, me and Nettie might be a little dark-skinned, but we spend a lot of time in the sun."

Tanner looked at him in confusion.

"I was joshin', Mr. Tanner," the half-breed said with another chuckle before growing serious. "Look, bein' half-Lakota, I've been dealin' with such hateful damn fools most of my life. Even more so since I married Nettie. Another Indian-hatin' white man won't make a difference."

After a bit of thought, Tanner nodded. "By the way, what're you doing at the house this early in the day? Shouldn't you be out watchin' over your cattle?"

"Me and the two boys were. Nettie saw you comin' and sent the two least ones, Pearl and Orville, out to get us."

"Makes sense."

"I'll send Jethro and Vin out to watch the cattle while us old-timers take our ease."

"Sounds like a right fine idea."

An hour before dusk, Tanner and Wilkins saw a rider coming. The half-breed stayed where he was, sitting in an old chair out front of the sod and wood house. Tanner slipped around the side of the building.

Barton stopped and dismounted, then stared at Wilkins, uncertain.

"What can I do for you, mister?"

"A peddler been here lately?"

"Can't say there has been." Over his shoulder, he called, "Nettie, bring our visitor some water."

Barton was shocked when the Osage came out, a crock of water in her hand. He did not move.

"Something wrong, Emmett?" asked Tanner, who had slipped around the corner of the building and come up behind Barton.

The newcomer whirled. "You!" he sputtered, shocked.

"One and the same. Now, what say you and me go into the barn and have us a nice little chat?"

"Hell with you." He went to mount his horse, but Tanner clubbed him down.

"We'll have none of that." Tanner bent, pulled Barton's pistol from the holster, and handed it to Wilkins. "Now, Emmett, let's go to the barn."

Barton looked like he was considering putting up a fight until he looked from Tanner to Wilkins and at the half-breed's two strapping sons. Head hanging, he headed toward the barn.

CHAPTER 11

"Why in hell has Whittemore been houndin' me all this time?" Tanner demanded after tying Barton to a pole. "Sand Creek was more than two and a half years ago."

"Hates you," Barton replied.

"I figured that. Why? I wasn't the only one that sat it out."

You were the only one to fight us instead of the Injuns." Barton's voice was bitter, but he cast a wary eye at Wilkins. "He lost his whole family to Cheyennes a while back. Women and children as well as the men. They were hacked up. He thought, like most of us did, that the Injuns should be paid back in kind."

"He wasn't the only one lost family that way."

"Nope, and that just made him more eager to punish those red devils."

"It was a peaceful camp under American protection."

117

"His family and many others never caused the Injuns any trouble, yet they were slaughtered and cut up, scalped, the women despoiled. We were just payin' them back. He was angry enough at Soule and Cramer for holdin' their men back, but when he learned that not only did you not take part, but you also actually tried to stop some of us from exacting our deserved vengeance, he was enraged. Swore he'd get you. He planned to court-martial you, but Soule thwarted that, so he's been doggin' you."

"With your help. And the others."

"Yep."

"Why didn't Whittemore just kill me? Or have you boys do it?"

"Wanted you to suffer, I reckon. Wanted you to be despised, hated by everyone — well, every white person — in the Colorado Territory." Again he looked nervously at Wilkins, who stood stone-faced.

"Even after the military report?"

"That angered him even more. Thought the Army had turned against him, ruined what he had hoped to be a long, glorious career. He blamed Soule, and when that son of a bitch was killed as he deserved, the lieutenant turned his attention to you." At Tanner's questioning look, he added, "You were Soule's pet."

Tanner shook his head in disbelief.

"Me and some of the other boys wanted to kill you, but he said no. He wanted everyone to know you were a coward, and worse, an Injun lover, and make sure you had to live with that."

"What if I had left the territory?"

"I ain't sure, but I think he would've killed you then. Don't really matter now."

"Why's that?"

"You're a dead man now. If I was you, I'd head back east if you want to keep yourself alive."

"Reckon not, Emmett. The one who should be heading back east is you."

"I ain't goin' anywhere."

"Not at the moment, you aren't. But later . . ."

Tanner wondered as he headed to the next stop on his travels in the morning whether he shouldn't have killed Emmet Barton instead of leaving him free, albeit in the hands of Charlie Wilkins and his two sons. Not only would it have removed one potentially deadly enemy, but it would also have prevented possible trouble for the half-breed and his family. He shook his head. It was too late now.

He had no trouble at his next stop and

pushed on, reaching the Hutton place late in the afternoon. As RJ Hutton moved to start unloading his supplies, Tanner stopped him. "You need to pay me for the goods," he said.

"After supper."

"It doesn't work that way, Mr. Hutton. You should know that. Even though this is the first time we've done this, Mr. Harker would have explained this to you when arrangements were first made for deliveries. Pay first, unload second. No money, no goods. Now, hand over what you owe, and we'll get to unloadin'."

Hutton scowled. He went into the house and returned, tossing a small sack that jingled when Tanner caught it. The deliveryman looked inside and counted the money. He pulled out a silver dollar and chucked it to Hutton. "That's overpayin', Mr. Hutton. Now, let's get to work." He added the money to a small, locked box in the front of the wagon and helped Hutton unload the goods.

Afterward, Tanner took care of the wagon and animals. At last, he sat down to supper with the family. It was another uncomfortable meal.

When they were done, Hutton said, "You can use the room in back." He had a gleam

120

of avarice in his eyes.

Tanner shook his head. "I'll sleep in the wagon." He was almost amused at the look of annoyance that crossed the homeowner's face. He had a fitful night's sleep on a pile of hay a few yards from the wagon, alert to the possibility that Hutton might try to rob him in the night.

As he drove the next day, Tanner wondered what Wilkins had done with Barton. He figured the half-breed or his sons would have escorted the veteran far from any of the other places Tanner was scheduled to visit. He hoped there would be no trouble.

He was jolted out of his ruminations when a bullet plowed into the wagon seat a few inches to his right, followed by the crack of a rifle a second later. He glanced behind him and saw two men racing toward him. Another slug tore through the wood of the seat and slithered along his ribs. He was glad neither had hit the mules, and the animals did not seem fazed.

"Damn!" The nearest rise he could hide behind was more than a hundred yards away, and he was not sure the mules were fast enough to get him there before the attackers were on him. He stopped the wagon and jammed the brake on, then grabbed his

121

rifle, jumped down, and slid under the wagon.

The riders had disappeared down a gulch, but moments later, they reappeared. Several more shots rang out, and Tanner realized the men were now shooting to take down the mules, whether to keep him from going anywhere or because of meanness, he did not know. Nor did he care.

"Try to shoot my mules, you sons a . . ." He fired twice quickly but hit nothing. More bullets came his way but with the attackers firing from racing horses, the men's shots were unsuccessful at hitting anything. Tanner cursed himself for having missed too. Although his targets were moving, he was not, so he should be able to do some damage. "Well, if you can shoot at my animals, I can damn well shoot at yours," he muttered.

He fired his fairly new .52-caliber Spencer repeater twice more. One of the attackers' horses went down, throwing its rider several feet over its head, then rolled over the man.

The other man jerked the reins so hard his horse almost sat on its haunches. As he tugged the animal around, Tanner placed two rounds in the mount. It fell, trapping the rider's leg.

With a deep breath, Tanner rose and started walking toward the men. As he walked, he pulled out the spring in the Spencer's buttstock and replaced the cartridges he had fired before pushing the spring back into place.

Tanner passed the first fallen horse and saw that the man under it was dead. He warily approached the second. That man was frantically trying to pull his leg out from under the horse's body. He sensed Tanner coming and scrabbled to pull his pistol.

"That is something I can't allow, Mr. Hutton," Tanner said, stepping on the man's gun arm. He knelt, and took the man's pistol, and stuck it in his belt. "Did you really think you could get away with robbin' me?"

"Nobody'd know. Harker would figure you'd run off with the money."

"Then you don't know Mr. Harker — or me — very well. He'd figure out soon enough that you'd killed me and took the money. He'd trace my travels, for one thing. For another, you're so damned stupid you'd likely go to town and start flashin' around money folks knew you shouldn't have. No, Mr. Hutton, you're a damn fool and a snake-eatin' puke."

"What're you gonna do with me?" Panic showed in Hutton's eyes.

"Well, let's see what my choices are." He

adopted a faux-thoughtful look. "I could just shoot you, I suppose. That would certainly keep you from trying this devilishness against anyone else. Or, well, I could just leave you here like this. You might be able to get yourself out from under the horse, though it's not likely, and if you did, it's a long walk back to your home. Reckon you would have a chance that way. On the other hand, if you can't get free, you'd be stuck here with no food or water under this terrible hot sun, just bakin' your brain. Oh, wait, if you had a brain, you'd not be in this predicament. Even so, it's not a pleasant way to go, though I guess there's no good way to go. Still, there are worse ways, and that'd likely be one of 'em."

"You could set me free and let me go," Hutton suggested hopefully, voice quavering in fear of being left here.

"So you can find another fella . . . who was your pal here, anyway?"

"My brother PJ."

"So you and some other lout could wait 'til I come by your place again and ambush me?"

"I wouldn't do that."

"Like hell, you wouldn't." Tanner rose, looking around as if a solution would pop up out of the ground. He was tempted to do either of the things he had mentioned, but he was no killer, or not a cold-blooded one. He would — and could — kill if it became necessary, but not like this.

Laying his Spencer down out of Hutton's reach, Tanner said, "I reckon you've seen your last delivery from Mr. Harker. When I get back to Kiowa, I'll send word to him. I reckon he'll talk to the law about you." He bent, grabbed the saddle horn, and tugged.

"Ain't no law gonna take the word of an Injun-lovin' coward."

Tanner's eyes flamed red. He released the saddle horn and stood. Without a word, he picked up his Spencer, Hutton's rifle and revolver, and his brother's two weapons and began walking back to his wagon, ignoring Hutton's screams of outrage and screeched demands for aid.

Angry, Tanner tossed the extra weapons into the wagon bed and climbed into the seat. He released the brake and clucked the mules into motion. Would it never end? he wondered.

His anger had quite a while to fester as he drove the empty miles to his two last deliveries and then back to Kiowa. Along the way, he decided that he needed to do something about Whittemore and the rest of his intolerable minions. He wasn't sure what he would do or where he would find the men who were spreading the pernicious rumors.

When Tanner reached Kiowa, Mort Jenkins, who ran the store in the town for Jabez Harker, told him he needed to make a trip to Denver to restock. It would be a few days, though.

Tanner nodded. While he wanted to get to Denver since it would be the best place to start looking for his antagonists, he wanted just as much to check on the Wilkins family.

The next morning, he rode out at a good clip, heading into the emptiness, and just before dark, he reached Charlie Wilkins' place. He dismounted, the door opened a crack, and the muzzle of a pistol eased out. "It's me, Charlie, Chase Tanner."

"Wasn't sure. Can't be too careful these days. C'mon in."

Tanner hung his hat on a peg near the door and sat at the table.

"You hungry, Chase?"

"Plenty."

Nettie did not need to be told. She began serving the supper she had been preparing.

"Orv, go tend to Mr. Tanner's horse."

"But what about supper?" the twelve-year-old said with a whine in his voice.

"It'll be here when you get done. Now

skedaddle."

"Yes, Pa."

Nettie served pork chops and potatoes with fresh bread, newly churned butter, and strong coffee. Tanner smiled. "Thanks." When she did not respond, Tanner looked at Wilkins. "Doesn't she ever talk?"

"Too much," the half-breed said with a laugh, "when there are no strangers around. She speaks well, too. Learned from the missionaries on the reservation."

"How'd you two meet, anyway?" the visitor asked as he dug into the food.

"I was doin' some scoutin' for the Army when I stopped by a friend's place on the Arkansas in what was Kansas Territory then. Met Nettie and was smitten. All this time later, here we are."

"You're a lucky man."

"Yep. So, what brings you here?"

"Came to see about Barton."

CHAPTER 12

"Barton won't be botherin' you or anyone else ever again," Wilkins said flatly.

"Can't say as I'm too upset. What happened?"

"Figured we'd feed him before escortin' him farther east on the Plains. Could be that he would use what sense he had left to keep on ridin' and doin' so fast, considerin' where he was. Or else maybe the Cheyenne or Kiowa would catch him. That would've been true justice."

"I take it plans did not go the way you wanted."

"Nope. First, he insulted Nettie, which did not endear the son of a bitch to me or anyone else here. Then he took the knife we had given him to cut his beefsteak and tried to kill Orville. Managed to cut the young fella a little before Vin clobbered him, as did Jethro a moment later. Before he knew what was happening, we had him tied face-down on his horse, and we were ridin' out to the east. Thought about shootin' him but decided that wasn't enough." He grinned viciously. "So we staked him out good and tight. He wasn't going anywhere after that."

Tanner nodded as he shoved another hunk of chop into his maw. "Take any bets on who or what got him first?"

"Nope. Didn't matter to us. We could ride on out there in the mornin' and see if we can tell from what there is left of him."

Tanner considered that for a moment. "Nah," he said with a shake of his head. "That was a couple weeks ago. Doubt there'd be anything left."

"My thoughts." The half-breed paused. "I don't very often break out the whiskey, but I'm willin' to do so in a salute to his memory."

"Well now," Tanner said with a grin, "that sounds appropriate. Only one, though. Or two if they're small. Nothing more."

"Agreed." Wilkins went to get the bottle.

The next morning, Tanner headed back to Kiowa, arriving in the just after dusk. The morning after that, he pulled out of town in the large freight wagon, pulled by six mules.

It took more than two days to reach the city, and Tanner pulled in late in the morning. After leaving the wagon and animals at the livery stable, he strode to Harker's store.

"Greetings, Chase," the owner said. "Mort sent word that you'd be coming. You're a little earlier than I expected, though."

Tanner just nodded. "I'm taking a few days."

"Sure," Harker responded, surprised. "Any particular reason?"

"Personal."

"If there's something bothering you that I should know about . . ."

Tanner shrugged.

"Did business go all right?" Harker sounded anxious as his employee handed him the box of cash. "Any trouble?"

Tanner hesitated, then nodded. "Haffner was decidedly unfriendly. Emmet Barton had talked to him just before I got there. And Hutton tried to kill me so he could rob me."

"No!" The store owner gasped. "Well, I'll speak to the sheriff right away about bringing him in."

"Likely won't be necessary."

"Why's that?"

Tanner explained, including why. "He might've gotten himself free and managed to get home, but I doubt it."

"Justifiable. Does the time you want for

personal business have anything to do with this?"

"It does. I aim to put an end to this nonsense of people trying to denigrate my name. Charlie Wilkins and I caught Barton, and I left him with Charlie. I figured they'd escort him somewhere he couldn't cause trouble, at least for a spell."

"And?"

"Wondered the same thing, so before I headed here, I visited Charlie. Apparently, Barton was stupid enough to try to kill Charlie's youngest son."

"I know Charlies Wilkins, and that would enrage him, and rightly so. He disposed of Barton, I assume?"

"He did in a way that was inventive and rather cruel, which the man deserved."

"Sounds like it. So what now?"

"I start looking for the others. I imagine they're here, or some of them are. At least it's a place to start looking."

"Take your time as you need, Chase. If you're going to take more than a few days, just let me know, and I'll get someone else to take the wagon down to Kiowa. Anything I can do to help, just ask."

"Appreciate it, Mr. Harker."

"Oh, I better warn you, Chase. There've been more reports that the Cheyennes and

Arapahos, along with the Sioux toward the north and the Comanches and Kiowas to the south, are getting more brazen and attacking along the trails and whatever outliers they can find."

"Doesn't mean much to me."

"It should make you wary. People here are not going to act very kindly to someone they've been told is an Indian lover. Step carefully."

"I will. Thanks for the warnin'."

"What'll you have, mister?" the bartender at the Pickax saloon asked.

"Beer." Tanner wondered why the man was staring at him.

"Hey, you're the one . . . ."

Tanner braced for trouble. The bartender saw it and grinned. "Noah Slater. You might not've seen me, but I was a member of D Company, Captain Soule's command."

"Thought you looked the littlest bit familiar. Were you one who agreed with Soule?" he asked warily.

"I was. 'Course, 'round here, it isn't wise to let that be known."

"Good thinkin'."

"You haven't been so lucky, have you?"

"That's one way of puttin' it."

Slater nodded and went off to get Tanner's beer, then set it in front of his customer. "It's on me. You were a corporal, as I recall?"

"Yep. Thanks." He lifted his glass in a salute, then took a healthy draft. "I'm tired of all the rumors and troubles they've brought and would like to put an end 'em."

"Can't blame you." Slater looked a little wary.

"You know where I can find Landis, Atkins, and the others? Or Whittemore?"

"No," the bartender said hesitantly. "Can't say as I do."

Tanner nodded. He took another gulp of beer and set the glass down. "Obliged for the beer. I'll not come in here again, Mr. Slater."

"It's not . . ."

"Good day, sir." Tanner walked outside and stood on the wooden sidewalk. He wondered what to do next. He had thought this would be easy. Ask around a little, and the men who hated him would show up. Of course, it was likely Slater had said nothing to him but would go running to one of the men he sought and told him Tanner was searching for him. "Should've kept your mouth shut, Chase," he muttered.

He wandered to the Silver Shovel saloon, got a beer, and sat at a table as far back as he could get. He sipped slowly, watching patrons come and go, but he saw no one he was searching for. He finally left and headed for a restaurant, thinking perhaps those he sought were not in Denver. They could be in one of the many flourishing mining towns or had even moved on, whether back east or to some other gold strike area like Montana Territory. He wondered if that might be a place for him to go, but he did not like running, which is what that would be to him.

After eating, he wandered around the city, searching for his nemeses, but he spotted none of them. As he was heading back to his hotel in the gathering dusk, someone hissed at him from an alley. He stopped, hand reaching for his Colt.

"No need for that," someone said quietly.

"Why the hell should I trust you, and just who the hell are you?"

"It's me, Noah Slater, Mr. Tanner. I have information for you."

"And you couldn't tell me before?"

"No. Come on out of the street."

Tanner did so, hand still on his revolver. It was dark in the alley, but he could see only the one man.

"I couldn't tell you before without riskin' my neck. There's folks 'round here who don't like people helpin' people they consider Injun lovers."

"That what you think?" Tanner asked harshly.

"Nope. If I did, I wouldn't be here now."

"You could be in cahoots with those boys."

"Reckon I could, but I ain't. You can believe me or not."

"So, what do you have to tell me?"

"Whittemore's gone back east. I don't think he intends to stay there, just visiting. I think he might be tryin' to get back in the Army's favor. Dexter Cobb and Aaron Pitts are in Georgetown, I hear, plyin' their trades. Cobb's a cobbler . . ."

"You're joshin', right?"

"Nope. Pitts is a tobacconist."

"What about Landis and Atkins?"

"Don't know about Landis. Ain't sure about Atkins, either, but I heard he was in one of the minin' towns."

"If no one is in Denver, why are you so scared of being seen talking to me?"

"There's other folks about who don't care for men like you . . . or what they think men like you are. They put up with boys like me because we were ordered not to take part in that damned massacre, but they think you voluntarily went against orders. I don't want them to think I'm collaborating with you."

"You are collaborating with me."

"All right, I don't want 'em to know I'm collaborating with you."

"Sounds reasonable. Thanks for the information, Noah, but remember this. If you're settin' me on the wrong path, somehow sendin' me into a trap or protecting those sons a bitches, I will hunt you down. That clear?"

"Yes, sir. I wish you good huntin' — for them, not me." Slater turned and slipped farther into the alley's darkness.

Tanner stood there for a few minutes, wondering whether he could trust the bartender. The man seemed honest, and Tanner did recall him being among the ranks of Captain Soule's men. Well, there was one way to find out, and that was to hunt down the men who had become his antagonists.

The next morning, Tanner saddled his horse and rode to Harker's store.

"Wanting to go back to work already?" the owner asked, surprised.

"Nope. Heading for Vicksburg and need some supplies."

"Sammy," Harker shouted, and the young man, who was still a laborer at the store, came running. "Give Mr. Tanner whatever he needs."

"Yes, sir."

Fifteen minutes later, Tanner was riding out of Denver, heading west. He got to within a few miles of Idaho Springs when he decided he did not want to risk staying in that city, so he pulled off the trail and made himself a small camp. Tending his mare and fixing a simple meal were dispensed with quickly, and he soon slid into his bedroll and was asleep.

After a simple breakfast, he was on the road. He was a little tense when he rode through Idaho Springs, but no one accosted him and he did not see Lisbeth, which had been one of his worries. Then he was outside the city and moving on. In the afternoon, he reached Georgetown. He stabled his horse at the livery, then found a room at a hotel. Not having eaten on the trail, he was hungry, so he stopped at a restaurant. After he finished his meal, he strode up the street, found the business he sought, and walked inside.

The owner, who was busy stocking a shelf with jars of pipe tobacco, called over his shoulder, "Be right with you."

The tobacconist froze when Tanner said, "Good afternoon, Mr. Pitts."

CHAPTER 13

"What do you want here, you co . . ." Aaron Pitts' quaking voice trailed off.

"I want you and your pals to leave me be and stop spreading false rumors about me."

"They're not false," Pitts said with insincere bravado.

"They are, and you damn well know it. I've put up with this for more than two years now. It's time for you boys to let it go and get on with your lives and let me get on with mine."

"I haven't done anything."

"Mr. Pitts, I am of a mind to shoot you down here and now, but I ain't that kind of man. However, if I get word that you are still spreading lies about me, I will have no compunction in putting a bullet in that empty head of yours. In fact, if I hear of any of you spreading lies about me again, I'll come for you first, seein' as how I know where you are. Of course, you could just pack up and head back east where you might be safe."

The tobacconist gasped. "That'd be dangerous."

"So will livin' here should you persist in trying to sully my name."

"But . . ."

"Where are the others?" Tanner asked, cutting him off.

"Don't know."

"You're lying again, Aaron. Unless Cobb has pulled out in the last day or two, he's here. Now, what about the others?"

"Other than the lieutenant headin' to the States to rejoin the Army or something and Dexter, I don't know anything about the others."

Tanner decided Pitts was telling the truth. "Just remember what I said. Now, let me see that jar of tobacco." Tanner pointed.

With some hesitation, Pitts pulled the jar off the shelf and handed it to Tanner. The latter opened it, sniffed it, and poured the contents on the floor. He grinned insolently. "Reckon you can sweep that up and put it back, though once your customers realize there's floor dirt mixed in, you might lose business. Nice talking to you, Aaron." Tanner strode out and headed for Cobb's cobbler shop.

The blood drained out of Dexter Cobb's face when he looked up to see who had entered his shop. "What?"

"Might need some new boots."

Cobb glanced down. "Those boots look fine to me."

"That might change when I kick you in the ass. Could foul one of 'em something awful."

Cobb gulped. "Why would you want to do that?"

"A little payback for spreading lies about me."

"I never . . ."

"Aaron said the same thing to me a few minutes ago, and I'll tell you what I told him: you're full of horse manure. I'm sick of my name being dragged through the mud, and I want it to stop now. If it doesn't, you'll be worm food." He started to head for the door but turned back. "Now that I think on it, I reckon your boots aren't worth a pig's fart. Just remember what I said."

"You're back sooner than I expected," Jabez Harker said when Tanner entered the store.

"Wasn't much business to take care of. I found two of 'em and warned 'em off." He sighed. "Maybe I'm a fool for not shootin'

140

'em, but I'm no killer. Not like that, anyway."

"Good. I'd hate for you to hang for doing away with those scoundrels."

"Would be rather inconvenient to lose an employee like that, wouldn't it?" Tanner asked with a laugh.

"Indeed it would. Probably have to pay for your funeral too, though I suppose a cheap pine box and a drunk gravedigger wouldn't cost that much." He laughed too. "So, are you ready to head back to Kiowa?"

"Reckon so. I'd like a couple bolts of cloth. A green one and a yellow, maybe."

Tanner looked at him in surprise. "Looking to make yourself a couple of bonnets or something?"

"No," Tanner said with a chuckle. "A gift for Nettie Wilkins. Charlie and the rest of the family helped with Barton, so I figured I'd get 'em all something. I'd guess, knowin' what little I do about women, that she'd like that."

"Reckon she would. What about the others?"

"Hell if I know. I reckon a girl Pearl's age would like a doll, though I have no idea what kind."

"Having experience with children and grandchildren, I can find one for you.

141

Orville's, what, twelve? Thirteen?"

"About that."

"Too old for little boys' toys, too young for men's things." He thought for a moment. "I reckon Charlie's already given him a rifle, but maybe a small pistol would be just the thing. I have a .31-caliber Colt Pocket revolver. It's old but was well taken care of. I took it in trade a while back from a fellow who was down on his luck. He never returned to get it."

"Sounds like a good deal. Now, what about Charlie and the two big boys?"

"There's a fine new saddle in back. Carson was making it for someone, but the fellow died, so I bought it. I think Charlie'd really like it."

"And his older sons?"

"I'm not sure. Let me think on it. Come around just after dawn with the wagon ready to go. We'll get you loaded up and on your way."

"See you tomorrow, boss."

"Wow, that is one fine saddle," Tanner when the wagon was loaded except for the gifts for the Wilkins family.

"Yes, sir, it is. Everything else is in that box." Harker pointed.

"For Charlie's sons?"

142

Harker grinned. "For each, a pair of tapa-deros and a pair of silver spurs, with over-sized rowels and some jingle bobs. Of silver, of course."

"I'm sure those young men will like 'em."

"I sent a rider down to Kiowa to tell Mort you're on your way. And to tell him this box and the saddle are yours."

Two and a half days later, Tanner rode into Kiowa and left the wagon for the work-ers there to unload. Before he could leave, Mort grabbed him. "Don't know why you took so long in Denver and don't care, but the families out there are expectin' sup-plies."

"And?"

"And I need you to head out soon's we finish unloading this wagon and load the smaller one."

"You can do all the loadin' you want, Mort. I'm not going anywhere today. If I can get some rest, I might be able to head out tomorrow."

"Mr. Harker will be mighty offended at your laziness."

"Mr. Harker will tell you the same thing I am: you want those supplies moved today, you can climb up on the wagon seat and get movin'."

"Just be here early in the mornin'."

"I'll consider it." Tanner mounted his horse, which had been tied to the back of the wagon, and pointed. "That box and the saddle are mine, as you were told. Keep 'em separate from the rest, and don't mess with them." He rode off.

He was glad to see his cabin was undisturbed, which he had worried about. He was glad to be home, but he could not get comfortable for too long.

In the morning, he rode into Kiowa. The smaller loaded wagon sat out front of Harker's store with the supplies covered by canvas.

"About time you got here," Mort Jenkins said.

"A word with you in private, Mort?"

"Oh, all right. But not long."

"Oh, this won't last long."

Jenkins led the way into the back room and turned to face Tanner. The latter slammed a fist into the former's stomach. Jenkins doubled over, gasping for air.

"You ever talk to me again like you did yesterday and a few minutes ago, and I will break several of your bones. You are not my boss. Mr. Harker is, and I've worked for him a lot longer than you have. You want to make an issue of things, you won't be as successful as you apparently think you'll be.

Now, get that saddle and my box loaded on the wagon."

Fifteen minutes later, Tanner rode out of the town, his horse tied to the back of the wagon. He had decided he would visit Charlie Wilkins last even though it meant adjusting his route. He hoped to spend a night with the family and see them enjoy the gifts he had brought.

He had no problems with any of his customers, as he had come to think of them, and had spent one night each with two families without rancor.

He finally reached the small Wilkins ranch mid-afternoon eight days after he had left Kiowa. He figured Wilkins and his two older sons were out with their cattle but would be home soon, so he waited. It was hot out in the sun, but he didn't feel right about knocking on the door. It might scare Nettie and the younger children.

To his surprise, an hour or so later, Nettie came out and handed him a cup of water. "Thanks, ma'am," he said but got no response as the woman went back into the house.

The three Wilkins men finally arrived. "Greetings, Chase," Wilkins said. Vin Wilkins took all three horses to the barn while Jethro and Charlie helped Tanner unload the family's supplies. As they worked, Wilkins said, "That's a damn nice saddle."

"Yep." He grinned. Wilkins looked at him in question, but Tanner said no more.

Finally, they had finished, the animals were tended, and they had sat down to dinner — beefsteak and yams. While the family was relaxing with coffee afterward, Tanner excused himself and headed out. He went to the barn and threw the box over one shoulder and the saddle over the other. At the door, he dropped the saddle and walked in with the box, which he sat on the table as everyone grabbed their coffee mugs.

"Christmas, if you celebrate that, has come a bit early this year," Tanner said as he opened the box. He grinned as he handed Nettie the bolts of cloth. As usual, she said nothing, but she grinned so hard Tanner thought her face might crack.

"And for you, Pearl, I have this." He handed the girl a porcelain doll.

She squealed in delight and rushed to a corner to investigate her new "companion."

"Orville, this is for you." Tanner gave the youth a box a foot square and four inches deep.

The boy took it, confused.

"Well, open it."

Orville did, and his eyes widened in wonder. "Look, Pa. My own revolver. A real one, with powder and balls and caps. It's . . . It's . . ."

"Just be careful with it," Tanner warned.

"Oh, I will, Mr. Tanner. Pa, can I take it out and look at it? Check it out?"

"Sure. Just make sure it ain't loaded."

"And these are for you," he said, looking from Vin to Jethro. He handed each a box.

Like eager schoolboys, they tore open their boxes, then joshed with each other in delight as they inspected their tapaderos and spurs.

Tanner closed the box and went outside, where he set it down. He picked up the saddle and went back inside. "This is for you, Charlie." He was shocked when he received a snarl instead of an expression of pleasure. "Something wrong?" he asked, perplexed.

"I can't take this thing, and I ain't so sure the rest of the family should take those other things you brought. This saddle is way too dear for a fella like me, and I don't abide charity."

"It's not charity. It's a gift for helpin' me out with Barton. Or, rather, taking care of Barton for me."

"This is too much for that. Gettin' rid of

147

him was as much for us as for you."

"I thought Indians were big on giving gifts to friends? Reckon I heard wrong. Well," he added after a sigh, "do with it what you will. Burn it, bury it, sell it, put it out in the barn and let it rot. Doesn't matter to me. Nettie, thank you for supper. I hope you and the rest of the family like the gifts." Angry, he headed for the barn. It would be well past dark by the time he got the wagon hitched up, but that didn't matter.

"Wait, Mr. Tanner!"

He turned, shocked. Nettie had never said a word to him, and now she was calling for him to wait? He was dumbstruck. "Yes, ma'am?"

"Men are fools," she said firmly as she marched up to him.

"Can't argue with that most times."

"Nettie, get back here, woman!" Wilkins bellowed from the doorway.

"When I'm ready. And when you act like you have sense." She turned back to Tanner. "Men have too much pride too often. Act crazy. Always try to butt heads like buffalo in rut. Women don't like it. Well, this woman doesn't like it."

"I appreciate your concern, ma'am, but your husband likely doesn't agree with you."

"I don't care."

"Dammit, woman, I said get back in the house," Wilkins roared, heading toward Nettie and Tanner. There was fire in his eyes.

Tanner's hand dropped to the butt of his Colt. "Get behind me, ma'am. This could get ugly."

CHAPTER 14

Charlie Wilkins took a step forward.

"Don't," Tanner said.

Jethro and Vin came out of the house to stand behind their father, one to each side. "What's goin' on, Pa?" the latter asked.

"Mr. Tanner is . . ."

Nettie stepped from behind Tanner. "Mr. Tanner is doing nothing wrong. I was tryin' to explain your foolish behavior to him, Charlie."

"It ain't foolish, and you got no need to explain anything to him. Now go back in the house."

"No. You two," she pointed at her sons, "go in the house. This is for your father and me to discuss with Mr. Tanner."

"Pa?" Vin asked.

Before Wilkins could answer, Nettie moved in front of him. "No arguin'. Just go."

"Pa?" Vin questioned again.

"Do it. I'll handle things here." Still looking at Tanner, he said, "Go on in, Nettie. Do like I said."

"No, Charlie." Her voice was soft, but there was defiance in it.

Wilkins raised his arm, ready to slap her. He topped when Tanner cocked his pistol. "Don't do it, Charlie. There's no call for hittin' her."

"This is my business, not yours."

"I won't abide you hitting a woman, especially your wife."

"You won't shoot me," Wilkins said, dropping his arm.

"Might, might not. It's for you to decide whether you think I will." Tanner uncocked and lowered his revolver but did not holster it. There were a few moments of silence, then Tanner asked, "What's gotten into you, Charlie?"

"None of your concern," Wilkins said.

"When you reject a gift I give you, practically throw me out of your house, and almost hit your wife, it does concern me."

With a shrug, Wilkins said, "No, it don't." He looked at Nettie. "Go on in the house, woman." His voice was softer.

"No. I want to make sure you two don't kill each other."

"You aimin' to shoot me, Chase?"

151

"Not unless I have to."

"And I have no pistol, woman." He paused. "It'll be all right. Go inside."

Nettie stood staring up at her husband for a few moments, then said, "One of you kills the other, I'll kill the one who's left." She slowly walked back to the house and went inside.

"Think she'd do it?" Tanner asked.

"Ain't sure, but I wouldn't put it past her."

"That's one tough lady."

"She's had to be to be able to put up with me — and condescending white men."

"That what this is all about? You think I'm a condescending white man?" When Wilkins nodded, Tanner asked, "What in hell makes you say that?" He was surprised but holstered his six-gun, no longer thinking he was in immediate danger.

"You bring gifts for us all. They're expensive. You expect something in return."

Tanner was shocked. "Sure, I expected something from you."

"See? Like I expected."

"I expected a thank you, nothing more. Like I said, you helped me out by taking care of Barton. It was a way of saying thank you to you and your family."

The half-breed said nothing, just looked uncertain.

152

"I might ask you for something someday, Charlie. And you could come to me asking for some help. If I asked, it'd be a friend asking a friend for help, not a condescending white man orderin' you to help me. And if you asked, I'd take it as a friend asking for help too, not a half-breed begging a white man for something."

It was hard to see with only the half-moon and some stars providing light, but Tanner thought Wilkins was thinking that over. Finally, he asked, "You really mean that, don't you?"

"I do." Then another thought hit him. "White men came 'round causing trouble?"

Wilkins hesitated. "A couple head of cattle missin', twice. Tracks lead me to think it's not Cheyenne or Arapaho or any other warriors."

"When?"

"First time was a little more than a month ago. Last time was almost three weeks."

"Just enough time for you to think they were gonna leave you alone."

"Yep."

"If they're on some kind of schedule, they should be showin' up in the next day or two. Well, night. I say we wait for 'em and ambush 'em when they show up."

"I can't ask you to do that, Chase."

"What did I just say about a friend helping a friend? Besides, you ain't asking, I'm offering."

"You sure you're all right with runnin' down your own kind?"

"If they're rustlin' cattle from a friend, they ain't my kind."

"Good." Wilkins sighed. "Well, I'd better go in and face the music." He didn't look happy.

"Rather fight off a dozen rustlers naked and unarmed, eh?" Tanner asked with a chuckle.

"Yeah," the half-breed said with a rueful smile. "She's a damn good woman, but there are times . . ." He laughed. "Those are generally the times I make a fool of myself. Like now." He paused. "Look, Chase, I . . ."

"No need to say anything. Just two old rams buttin' heads over a misunderstandin'."

They entered the house, and Nettie and the rest of the family looked up, worried. They breathed sighs of relief at the sight of the two men.

"About time you two got back," Nettie said. "The family's hungry for my peach cobbler and have had to wait while you two were out there arguin' over something that was unimportant. Now sit."

Cobbler and coffee were dished out and they all ate happily, everyone praising Nettie for her tasty dessert. When it was over, the two young children went into the other room while the two older ones went outside to make sure the horses had hay and water.

When they closed the door, Nettie turned to her husband. "You just wait 'til we're alone, Charlie Wilkins. I'll certainly give you a piece of my mind."

"I'd rather have a piece of . . ." Wilkins said with bravado but slammed his lips shut at the look the woman gave him.

"Don't go too hard on him, Nettie. Like you said, men are fools. Some more than others." He grinned. "He just had a mix-up about things."

Tanner spent the next two nights with Wilkins and one of his older sons, riding among the cattle, watching, waiting. When they got back to the house and were eating, Tanner said, "I can only afford another couple nights before I have to head back to Kiowa, Charlie."

The half-breed nodded. "Can't expect you to spend the rest of your days waitin' to catch some rustlers. Good chance they won't even be back."

"They will be, I'm pretty sure. Once men like that get away with it, they figure they can do it anytime. Have you heard of 'em hittin' any other places?"

"No, but I don't have much contact with the other ranchers or farmers. Most of 'em don't trust a breed."

"You think it might be one of them rustlin' your cattle because you're a half-breed?"

"I've considered it. I just don't know. I wouldn't doubt it, though."

"If we manage to catch 'em, do you want me to bring 'em to Kiowa to face justice? When I left, there still wasn't any official law around, but we could find a judge somewhere, I suppose."

"That'd be foolish."

"Why?"

"They'd just claim I was the one rustlin' cattle, and they were tryin' to catch me when you apprehended 'em. You think the law's gonna believe a half-breed over white men?"

"Nope, but wouldn't the townspeople wonder why I apprehended the men?"

"You thought they might be rustlers, even though they said they weren't."

"So there's only one option."

"Yep. You still willin' to help?"

"Well, I don't cotton to killing men in cold blood, but men stealin' cattle from a friend is a different tale."

With only the stars for light it was difficult to see, but Tanner caught movement to his left and slid out of the saddle. In the darkness, anyone looking this way likely would see only another animal, not a man in a saddle.

He walked slowly toward the movement, tugging his mare along. He finally spotted a man lassoing a steer, preparing to lead it away. Then he saw another doing the same. He hoped they were the only two, but he couldn't be sure, and he couldn't figure out how he was going to get both men. It was too dark for a good shot, and he couldn't get close to both at the same time. Nor could he risk shouting for Wilkins or Vin, the son on watch with them tonight.

Suddenly the man to his right disappeared from his saddle. With the light breeze and the soft noises the animals made, he heard nothing from the spot where it had happened. Then came a gunshot.

"Jed?" the other man called. "Jed! What's goin' on?"

Tanner decided he could not wait. He leaped into his saddle and began pushing his way through the small herd. The rustler saw him coming, dropped the rope with which he had lassoed the steer, and turned tail and fled. Tanner kicked his horse into a lope behind him.

A horseman loomed up in front of the rustler, and a shot rang out. Tanner was glad he had not been shot since he was fairly close behind the fleeing man. That fellow veered to his right, and Tanner followed. The latter galloped off at an angle and was able to eat up the distance between them quickly.

Two more gunshots spat into the night but apparently did not hit the rustler.

Tanner pulled up alongside the man and matched his racing horse against the rustler. He pulled his Colt and shot the man in the side, then again. The man reeled in the saddle and finally fell.

Tanner pulled to a stop and turned back, then dismounted and knelt beside the rustler. Vin Wilkins came riding up and stopped. "You damn near killed me with that first shot, Vin."

"Sorry, Mr. Tanner," the young man said sheepishly.

Moments later, Charlie Wilkins trotted up. "Got the bastard, I see. He ain't dead yet, though."

"He will be before long," Tanner said. "You get the other one?"

"Yep."

"You're sure there were only two?"

"Pretty sure," Wilkins said. "Haven't heard anyone ridin' off."

"Good." Tanner stood. "This one'll be dead by the time we tie him to his horse. You know either of 'em?"

"Don't know the other one." He dismounted and checked the one who lay dying. "Not this one either. What're we gonna do with 'em?"

"Take 'em to Kiowa. Maybe somebody'll claim 'em."

"Might cause trouble. People'll be askin' questions."

Tanner thought that over. "What do you suggest?"

"Take 'em some miles farther out on the prairie and dump 'em. Wolves, vultures, coyotes, and bears'll take care of cleanin' up the mess."

"Suppose somebody finds 'em first?"

"They'll find two bodies with bullet holes in 'em and no evidence of who did it. If they have any decency, they'll bury the bodies. If they know the area, they'll know it'll take 'em a couple days to get to Kiowa, and the bodies'll be pretty ripe before they get there.

If they don't know the area, they'll likely just leave 'em there. Maybe tell someone in Kiowa if they get there. Or Denver."

"We're right close to your place."

"We'll head north and maybe a little west. That'll put them within a few miles of Gibson's place rather than here."

"Sounds good. Let's go."

"You can go on back to the house. Nettie will feed you, and you can get some sleep. You can take off just after it's light. Like you said yesterday, you need to get back to Kiowa."

Tanner mounted and nodded. He started to ride slowly but turned back at Wilkins' voice.

"Thanks, Chase."

Tanner nodded, touched the brim of his hat, and rode off.

CHAPTER 15

Tanner saw a slight movement ahead in the snow and brought his wagon to a halt. When he realized it was a person, not an animal, he drove closer, stopped again, and jumped down from the seat. He knelt next to the person — he learned it was a woman when he rolled her onto her back. She wore no blanket or other outer garment against the elements, being clad only in her buckskin dress. She was nearly frozen. He stood and looked around through the lightly falling snow. There was no indication of anyone else in the area. "Where the hell did you come from, woman?" he muttered. He shrugged. He didn't know what to do with her, but he could not just leave her here to die, even if she was an Indian.

He carefully picked her up and set her in the wagon bed, then stood thinking. Finally, he shrugged, took off his heavy bearskin coat, and tucked it around her, barely leaving her face uncovered so she could breathe. He donned the town coat he kept in a box behind the seat and climbed aboard. "Let's go, mule," he said, snapping the reins. "She needs shelter, and this coat won't keep me warm for long."

Three hours later, he pulled up in front of his small cabin a couple of miles outside Kiowa. Though he was shivering, he brought the woman in and deposited her on his creaky bed. He covered her with blankets, took off his town coat, put on his bearskin coat, and quickly got a fire going in the stove. Despite being tired and cold, he headed outside to unhitch the wagon, tend to the mule, and put it inside the barn, making sure it and his horse had hay and water.

But his work was not yet done. Inside, he removed his coat, hung it on a peg next to the door, and heated up some frozen buffalo stew he had brought back from town before he left on his latest rounds. Finally, he plunked his tired body in a chair and ate hungrily while wondering about the woman and what to do with her.

Tanner was sitting at his table when a gasp from the woman made him spin in his chair. He rose and hurried to the bed. The woman gasped again, this time in fear when she saw a white man looming over her.

"I ain't gonna hurt you, Miss," he said hastily. It did not calm her. "Are you hungry?" The only response he got was wide-eyed fright. "Do you speak English?" Again, he got no response. With a sigh, he went to the fire, filled a bowl with stew, and went back to the bed, where the woman still cowered. He knelt and directed a spoonful toward her mouth. She shrank back, getting as far from him as she could.

"I'm not gonna hurt you," he repeated. "This is good. It'll make you feel better." He ate the spoonful, then another. "See?" He waited silently, trying to suppress his frustration.

"You're safe here," he said quietly after a minute or two. "You're warm and there's food, and I'm not gonna hurt you or even touch you. Now, come on and eat a little."

With frightened eyes, she tentatively leaned forward and let him feed her the spoonful of stew.

"Good?" he asked with a smile.

She said nothing but allowed him to feed her more. She relaxed a little, but she was still wary. "Want some coffee?" he asked after a few minutes.

He had to be satisfied with a cautious nod. He handed her the bowl and went to the fireplace, then filled a tin mug with coffee, added a dose of sugar, and returned to the bedside. He handed her the cup and took the empty bowl. "Do you speak English?" he asked again.

She offered a short nod.

"What's your name? I'm Chase Tanner."

"Cloud Dancer," she said softly, her voice quavering with lingering fear as well as the cold that still resided deep inside her.

"Pretty name. Fitting for a pretty girl. You Cheyenne or Arapaho?"

"Cheyenne." She burrowed a little deeper into the blankets, shivering.

"I found you half-froze in the snow a few hours away and brought you here. Your clothes were icy, and now they're wet. You really should get them off and let 'em dry."

Horror leaped onto her face.

"I ain't gonna look. I'll go outside and see to the animals, maybe get some more wood for the fire while you take those wet clothes off. You wrap yourself up good in these blankets. I got an old shirt and pair of pants over there if you want to put those on. I'll knock before I come back in and wait for you to say you're ready. That sound all right?"

Cloud Dancer shook her head vigorously.

"You can't stay in these wet clothes. You'll

get mighty sick. I'll put up some rope so you can hang them near the stove."

She still looked uncertain and scared. He took the empty coffee cup from her and placed it on the table. He got an old shirt and trousers and put them on the table as well. Then he hung some rope near the fire. "I'm going out now. You'll be all right. Just hang your dress and leggings, if you're wearing 'em, near the fire." He pulled on his bearskin coat, and with a shrug, he went outside.

He made sure the horse and mule were warm enough in the barn, gathered some firewood from the stack, and carried it to the cabin, where he placed it just to the left of the door and covered it with a canvas tarp. He had taken his time at it, but he gave her more time. Watching the falling snow, he wondered again how the woman had come to be where she was. Then, with a sigh, he knocked on the door. He got no answer, so he tried again. Again, there was no answer. Reluctantly he edged the door open. He waited before entering, surveying the room. He could not see her. His clothes were gone from the table and hers were hanging on the rope, but she was not in the bed. He smiled. "I don't think it's a good idea to attack me, Cloud Dancer. One of us might get hurt. Now toss away whatever you're planning to hit me with and come on out where I can see you."

A log landed with a thump a few feet from the door, then Cloud Dancer came into view. She was dressed in his clothes, the pants held up by a piece of rope, the shirt hanging to her knees. Tanner couldn't help but laugh. "You are a sight, Cloud Dancer." He chuckled as he walked inside, then grew more solemn. "You want to talk or get some more sleep?"

"Need sleep." The voice was quiet, but it could not hide the fear.

"You needn't worry. Go on to the bed." He blew out the candles, then settled on the floor, pulling the heavy coat over him and resting his head on his saddle. He was out quickly, but he slept lightly.

In the morning, Tanner stoked the fire, made bacon, and heated coffee. He was sitting at the table with some of each when the aroma woke Cloud Dancer. She looked over at him with a combination of hunger and fear. "There's plenty," Tanner said with a smile. "I ain't feeding you this morning. You can feed yourself. Plate and cup are over next to the stove."

The woman rose and cautiously headed to the stove, giving the man as wide a berth as she could. She got food and coffee and hurried back to the bed, where she ate hungrily.

"Feeling better?" Tanner asked.

"Little."

"Good. I reckon your clothes are dry by now. Soon's I finish eatin', I'll go outside for a bit so you can get changed."

"All right."

Soon after, Tanner donned his coat and left. He made sure the animals had feed and brought more firewood to the cabin. Thinking the Cheyenne should not have taken that long to get ready, he knocked on the door.

"All right to come in." The woman's voice came from inside.

He opened the door carefully, but the woman was sitting at the table with a cup of coffee in front of her. Tanner joined her. "What happened, Cloud Dancer?"

She said nothing for a little while, which had Tanner thinking she wasn't going to talk about it. Then she said, "Family was travelin' back to village after visiting friends. White men attacked us. Killed everyone, I think, except me. I ran."

"Didn't they follow you? There should have been tracks in the snow to follow."

"Not sure they followed, but snow was

fallin' hard. Covered tracks fast."

"Makes sense. The snow was coming down pretty heavy there for a while. But what about a blanket or something? You had none when I found you."

"I thought men were chasin' me. After runnin' for some time, I fell. When I got back up, the wind blew my blanket away. I thought I heard men followin', so I ran again."

"I'm sorry for you, Cloud Dancer. No one should go through that."

"You're maybe the only white man who feels that way."

"Could be." He paused. "So, what am I gonna do with you?"

"Whatever you want." It was said with resignation.

"If you think I'll take advantage of you, don't worry. I won't do that."

"You are a strange white man."

Tanner shrugged. "Not my way to take advantage of any woman. Well, you can stay here a few days, let yourself recover a bit more, then we can figure out what to do. I expect you'd like to return to your people."

"Yes," she said, her voice wistful.

"I don't know how we could arrange that, but I'll give it some thought."

"Thank you," Cloud Dancer whispered.

The pounding on the door startled Tanner. "Over there, Cloud," Tanner ordered in a low voice, pointing to the front corner to the left of the door. Unless the door was fully open, she would not be seen. He pulled out his Colt and held it down alongside his leg. He opened the door. "Can I help you?" he asked, appraising the two men standing outside and noting there was a saddled third horse.

"Mind if we come in?"

"I do."

"Ain't very neighborly of you."

"I ain't a neighborly sort of fella. I don't know you, and I ain't very friendly with men who come poundin' on my door for no reason."

"Need to get out of the cold for a bit."

"Kiowa is only a couple miles that way," Tanner said, pointing.

"Actually, we're trackin' a Cheyenne. A woman. Thought she might be here."

"Why would you think that?"

"You're the only place around, and we thought we saw some wagon tracks."

"I ain't the only one with a wagon."

"Look, mister, we won't abide a man

hidin' an Indian. Now let us in there to check. You're tellin' the truth, we'll be on our way."

"No. What you're gonna do is get the hell off my property and leave me alone."

"You leave us no choice." He started to push his way inside.

CHAPTER 16

Tanner brought his Colt up, cocking it as he did, and fired. The slug tore through the man's belly and out the back, hitting his companion behind him. Both fell. Tanner caught movement to his left and figured it was a third man. He dropped to one knee, poked his head around the door, and put a lead ball into the chest of a man who was charging toward the door. "Stay here, Cloud," he ordered, then slipped outside and circled the cabin to make sure there wasn't a fourth man.

"You . . . you . . . killed three white men to protect me?" Cloud Dancer asked, incredulous.

"Yep."

"Why?"

"Should I have turned you over to them?"

"Most men — white men — would."

"We've already established I ain't like most white men."

The woman shook her head, still not believing he had done this.

"Will you be all right by yourself for a while?"

"I think so." Fear had crept back into Cloud Dancer's voice. "Why?"

"Need to get rid of these bodies."

"What about their horses?"

"I'll figure out something."

Tanner hitched up the wagon, then tossed the three bodies into the bed. He tied the dead men's horses to the rear of the wagon and pulled out. He headed northeast away from Kiowa for a couple of miles, then turned northwest. Two hours later, he dumped one body. Half an hour later, he dumped a second one, then the third about the same distance away. The snow had stopped late yesterday, but the leaden sky indicated it would begin again soon. Tanner figured the new snowfall — if heavy enough, which he thought it would be — would cover the bodies even if scavengers had ravaged them. With any luck, they wouldn't be discovered 'til spring. Another thirty or forty minutes of zigzagging through the crusted snow, and he was shed of two of the men's saddles and other tack. He untied two of the horses and sent them running with swats on the rump. There was little to distinguish them from a thousand other horses, so even if they wandered back to Kiowa, they likely wouldn't be identified as belonging to the men Tanner had killed. He would keep the third. It would come in handy if he had to move Cloud Dancer.

He was exhausted when he returned to his cabin well after dark, but he unhitched the wagon and tended the animals. Finally, he headed into the cabin. A flash of fear crossed Cloud Dancer's face, then relief. "Sit," she said. In minutes, she had stew and coffee in front of Tanner.

"Thanks." He was surprised she had done so, but he welcomed it, as he did the second serving of both.

When he had finished, Cloud Dancer said, "You rest now."

"You gonna hit me over the head and run away?" he asked with a feeble smile. When a look of horror spread across her face, he said, "I'm joshin', Cloud." He was relieved by her look of relief.

"Oh. You take bed," she added as he headed toward the past couple of night's sleeping spot on the floor.

"You sure? It doesn't seem right some-how."

"Take bed," she commanded.

"Yes, ma'am." Less than two minutes

later, he was asleep.

A week went by with no sign of trouble, then another. During that time, Cloud Dancer relaxed more each day, much to Tanner's pleasure. However, he began to worry about work. Though freighting had slowed down with the weather so bad, he was nearly due to pick up a load of supplies in Denver for the mercantile in Kiowa and then deliver to the area ranchers and farmers, but he did not know what to do about the Cheyenne. He could not leave her here alone for the week or so it would take to get his business done in Denver and get back; it was too dangerous. Nor could he take her to Denver. The only choice, it seemed, was to try to get her back to her people. That could take weeks — if he even lived through it.

He explained that to her, but she seemed sad, which made Tanner wonder. "I thought you wanted to go back to your people?"

She shook her head. "I changed mind."

"Why?"

"Goin' back is bad for me. Little food. Movin' all time. Fightin'. Not safe." She hung her head. "And I like you," she said shyly.

The latter surprised him even more. "I

174

like you too. Very much." As he said it, he realized he meant it. He wondered how the feeling could rise up in so short a time, but there was something about her that drew her to him. He didn't think it was love, but it might not be far off. He wondered even more how she could've come to like him in such a short period, especially considering how they had met.

He took a look at her as if seeing her for the first time. She was fairly tall for a woman and slender, though amply curved. Her hair was long, pitch-black, and silky, almost waist-length. Her face was long and angular, and he thought her beautiful. Her skin was fairly dark, her cheekbones high, her eyes coal-black. She had shown herself to be a good cook, though some of the pots and pans and such were strange to her, especially the stove. She kept the cabin clean, and she was diligent about her own cleanliness.

For another day or two, he considered the quandary, then hit upon an idea. "You remember what I told you about not bein' able to leave you here or outside Denver or anyplace?"

"Yes." She sounded wary and worried.

"Well, I got a friend you could maybe stay with. He's one of the people I deliver supplies to from time to time. If I take you there, I can get to Denver and back, then pick you up again when I bring supplies to the ranchers out that way."

"You trust I stay with another man alone?"

"No, no, it ain't like that. He's married to an Osage woman. They have four children."

"Oh, that all right, maybe."

"We'll leave in the morning."

"You sure he'll let me stay?"

"Ain't completely sure, but I reckon he and Nettie won't have a problem with you stayin' there."

As they were preparing to leave the next morning, Tanner asked, "You prefer ridin' a horse with a white man's saddle or ridin' in a wagon?"

"Ride horse."

Nettie cautiously opened the door after Tanner knocked. When she saw who it was, she grinned and opened the door wide. Tanner saw her uncock a small revolver and slip it into the pocket of her calico dress.

Tanner and Cloud Dancer sat at the table, and Nettie served them coffee. "Pie?" she asked. "Supper soon, so no eatin' your meal now."

"That sounds good, Nettie."

The Osage served them and sat on Tanner's side of the table so she could look at Cloud Dancer. "What is your name?" she asked.

"Cloud Dancer." It was said shyly.

"You have a white name?"

"No."

"I call you . . ." Nettie thought, then nodded. "I call you Elmira."

"Funny name," the Cheyenne said with a giggle.

"So is Nettie, but I like." She smiled and turned to Tanner. "Is she your woman?"

"Well," Tanner stuttered, "I ain't quite sure." Seeing the hurt look in Cloud Dancer's eyes, he hastily added, "But it's moving that way. I think I'd like that, but we haven't known each other long."

"She'd make you a good woman."

"How can you tell that? You just met her."

"Women know such things." She smiled when the newly named Elmira nodded. "Why are you here?"

"I'll explain that when Charlie gets back. Better to do it once instead of twice."

"Ah, men. Never understand 'em." She laughed.

Tanner shook his head. He and pretty much every other man would never understand women. One of life's great mysteries was that opposite genders needed each other but often had little understanding of the other.

He paid little attention to the small talk the two women made. "You like the pistol I brought you a while back time, Orville?" he asked the boy, who was sitting in a corner whittling something. "I forgot to ask before."

"Yes, sir. Pa's even took me out a few times to show me how to shoot it and load it and clean it too."

"Cleanin' it and knowin' how to load it are good things."

"Yep. I'm runnin' out of powder, though."

"Well, considering it's been a few months, I ain't surprised. I'll see about bringing some more next time."

"Would you?" Orville asked, wide-eyed.

"Yep."

Minutes later. Wilkins walked in, took off his short, heavy blanket coat, and hung it on a peg. When he turned back to the room, Cloud's Dancer's face lost much of its color, and she gasped.

"What's wrong, Cloud?" Tanner asked, confused and worried.

"He bad," she managed to murmur.

"No, he ain't. He's a good man." Tanner was even more confused, and Wilkins stood in the doorway dumbstruck.

"He Crow."

"You know him?" Tanner asked.

"No. He bad. Crow." Her breathing was ragged.

Tanner and Nettie came around the table and sat at her sides. Tanner placed an arm protectively around her; Nettie held one of the Cheyenne's hands.

"Somebody want to tell me what in hell's goin' on?" Wilkins demanded. He sat at the table across from the three. "I'm not gonna hurt you, girl. I'm not a bad man."

"You Crow. Bad."

"No, I'm Lakota, and only half-Lakota. You're Cheyenne?" When she nodded, he said, "Lakota and Cheyennes are friends. I'm half-white too, and I have little to do with my mother's people anymore. Not since she died." He paused. "Look, miss . . . What's your name?"

"Elmira," Nettie answered for her.

"Look, Miss Elmira, I don't know why you think I'm a Crow. My people and yours are friends. Live together, fight together. You just met Nettie, but do you like her?"

Elmira nodded, fright still deep in her eyes.

"Do you think she would be married to a bad man?"

"No," Elmira said hesitantly.

179

"Why do you think he's a Crow?" Tanner interjected.

The Cheyenne pointed to Wilkins' neck. Wilkins reached up and touched the choker — a beaded image of a dark bird — he wore. He laughed. "This? I got this off a Crow I killed in a battle some years ago. I thought it looked fancy and have been wearin' it ever since."

"You do not lie?"

"Nope." Seeing that she was still frightened, he smiled and yanked off the beaded choker. With it in hand, he walked to the stove, opened the door, tossed the offending item into the flames, and closed the door. He sat back down. "No more Crow. Just Lakota."

Relaxing, Elmira nodded.

"Good. Now, Chase, what brings you and this fine young woman to our house?"

Tanner explained the situation. "Since she doesn't want to go back to her people, I thought you and Nettie might let her stay here a spell while I was makin' the trip to Denver and back, then bringing goods to the farmers and ranchers out here. I'd make you the last stop and take Cloud Dancer back to my cabin, then do it all over again whenever I had to make trips."

"Nettie?" Wilkins asked.

"If you say no, I slap you."

Wilkins grinned. "I bet you would, woman." He grew more serious. "Do you want to stay here, Elmira? Now that you know I'm not a Crow, you don't need to be afraid of me."

"You not hurt me?"

"Oh, no. I wouldn't do that." His face wrinkled as he thought. "You know Chase and I are friends, right?"

She nodded.

"And you like Chase?"

Another nod.

"So, do you think Chase would bring a woman he cares for to a place where she would be in danger?"

"No," Elmira whispered.

"I welcome you and would like to have you stay, but only if you'd like to. If you're scared of me, then it's best you do not stay. But I promise I won't hurt you."

"And them?" Elmira pointed at Jethro and Vin, who had come in just before Tanner explained. He had seen the looks of desire in their eyes but had dismissed them.

"They won't bother you. Right, boys?"

"Yes, Pa."

Tanner did not think they sounded all that sincere.

Neither did Nettie. "You touch Elmira,

181

I'll throw you out, even though you're my sons. Send you away with nothing. No food, no weapons, nothing."

"You won't do that, Ma," Vin said with a cocky smile.

"Is my home. Elmira is guest, and she is Chase's woman." It was only a little lie. "If I don't throw you out, you have to fight Chase."

"And me," Wilkins said.

The young men blanched. "Understood, Ma," Jethro said for both.

Tanner stared at them and decided they meant it.

"Now," Wilkins said, "it's up to you, Elmira. If you want to stay, we'd like to have you. You'll be safe here, and Nettie will make sure you're all right. So, do you want to stay?"

Elmira looked at Tanner, who nodded and smiled.

"I stay," she said, her voice stronger.

CHAPTER 17

"You're an Injun lover, Tanner. What do you say about these attacks?"

"What did you say?" Tanner looked square at Horace Fleming, the baker in Kiowa. He was at a meeting of townsmen to discuss the Indian problem months after he had found Cloud Dancer.

"You heard what I said." Fleming sneered.

"No, I saw your mouth open, and your lips moved, but all that came out were clumps of mule manure."

The baker's eyes bulged.

"You know the Indian raids are gettin' close to some of our farms out there on the prairie, don't you?" said Ed Crismon, one of the farmers to whom Tanner brought supplies.

"So I've heard."

"That don't worry you?"

"Some. You know damn well I'm out there by myself quite often, making deliveries to you and the others."

"He's just saying that 'cause he's an Injun lover," Fleming jeered.

Tanner ignored him.

"I heard he's even got a squaw staying at his place," Fleming added.

"That true?" asked Clark Clarkson, who owned the hardware store in Kiowa.

"Nope." It wasn't a lie. Elmira was with the Wilkins family as he prepared to make a trip to Denver. He had been in town making arrangements when he'd heard about the meeting and decided to stop in the Mud Puddle saloon. The place was crowded since Kiowa had grown considerably this spring.

"I think we ought to go take a look," someone in the crowd snapped.

"Look all you want, boys, but you touch so much as one stick of firewood, and I'll put a bullet in you."

"He's just tryin' to scare us into not goin' out there," another man said.

"I think we should go out there right now," came another voice.

"What do you say, Tanner?" Clarkson asked.

"Have at it, boys. You know where my cabin is. My warning still stands, though. I'll gut-shoot any man who damages my property."

"Let's go, boys," Fleming said. He sounded eager.

"You'll be stayin' here, Tanner," Clarkson said.

"Fine, long as you buy me a beer."

More than half the men stomped out. Tanner sipped the beer that was provided. He was outwardly calm, but he hoped Elmira had not left anything from her people around. They had tried to make sure of that, but one could never tell. It was possible something had been overlooked.

Two hours later, the men returned, looking triumphant. "What's this?" Fleming demanded, holding up a calico dress.

"It's a dress. You lose a few pounds, Horace, it'll probably fit you. Bet you'd look good in it, too."

Laughter spread across the room, and a pink tint spread across Fleming's face. "It shows you have a woman living there. An Indian woman, I'd wager."

"You ever seen an Indian woman wearing such a dress? Hell, have you ever even seen an Indian woman?"

"Then where's it come from?" Crismon asked. "I don't reckon it's yours." He smiled.

"It's too small for me even should I decide I wanted to wear it. I had me a doxy from

185

Denver staying at my place for a spell."

"That would explain it," Clarkson said. "Sorry, Chase."

Tanner shrugged. "It's all right. But there's one other thing." He lifted his beer, walked two steps, and punched a man square in the face with the mug. His other hand darted out and snatched a pouch from where it was sticking out of the man's vest as the victim staggered back a few steps.

"What the hell, Chase?" Chrismon asked.

"This is mine," Tanner said, holding up the pouch. "Money I've worked hard for, risked my neck for." He shoved it into his pocket. "And I told you what I'd do to anyone who messed with my belongings." He drew his Colt.

Several men stepped between him and his victim. "Can't have any of that," Clarkson said. He smiled weakly, afraid. "Besides, you said you'd shoot anyone who damaged your property, not someone who 'accidentally' picked up a sack and stuck it in his vest while lookin' around."

"You're splittin' hairs, Clarkson, but I'll let it pass this time. Now, if you'll excuse me, I'll let you boys finish discussin' what to do about your Indian problem, though you didn't seem to be getting anywhere with it." He set the beer mug on the bar and pushed past Clarkson, stopping in front of the man who had stolen his money. He didn't know his name. The man's face was covered with blood from his shattered nose, and he looked woozy. "Keep away from me, boy, if you value your life." He pushed the man out of his way, grabbed the dress out of Fleming's hands, threw it over his shoulder, and left.

From the saloon, he went straight to Harker's store. "I want the wagon hitched and loaded by daylight, Mort," he said in a voice that indicated he would allow no argument.

The storekeeper saw the look in Tanner's eyes and decided to hold his tongue, other than to say, "It'll be ready."

Back at his cabin, Tanner took a deep breath and let it out. This was not a good development. If the Cheyennes and Arapahos were indeed raiding near the outlying farms and ranches, things could get bad and quickly. He would have to think about how to protect Elmira. Leaving her at Charlie Wilkins' place no longer seemed to be a good choice. It might only bring trouble for the Wilkins family.

Around mid-morning two days later, Tanner pulled into Denver and halted in front

187

of Harker's store. The owner came out as Tanner hopped down off the seat. "Welcome back, Chase."

"Glad to be here."

"Come on in. I'll have someone take care of the wagon and animals."

They went to the back room Harker used as an office. They sat, and a salesgirl poured them coffee. Harker took a sip, then said, "You look troubled, Chase. Something bothering you?"

"Folks in Kiowa are saying Indians are raiding closer to the farms and ranches out beyond the town."

"I've heard the same thing. Could be bad for business." When Tanner raised an eyebrow at him, he added, "And for the people. Business is always on my mind. It has to be."

"Reckon so. But it could mean danger for a lot of folks, includin' Charlie Wilkins, if it's true. And since he's a half-breed and Nettie's an Osage, it could get dicey if people learn that. Other farmers and ranchers might go after them."

"I hate to say it, Chase, but there's not much, if anything, I can do about that."

"I know. I'm gonna warn him and see what he wants to do. But that presents a problem for me too."

188

"How so?"

"I'm in love with a Cheyenne woman."

Harker almost spat coffee across his desk. "Tell me you're joking, Chase." But he knew it was the truth; Tanner would not joke about such a thing. "How'd you ever fall in love with a Cheyenne? How'd you even meet a Cheyenne woman?"

Tanner explained how he had found Elmira Cloud Dancer starving and half-frozen. "I've been leaving her with Charlie's family when I come here and when I do my rounds. I take her with me on some of the stops I make, ones where I'm not gonna spend the night, takin' her back to Charlie's in between. I leave her half a mile away, hiding among trees along a stream or something while I ride up to the house and make my delivery. It scares the hell out of me to do so, but this way, we can be together for a time."

"Not the best way to have a relationship."

"That's a fact. And somehow word has gotten out — well, it's just rumors yet — that I'm living with a squaw. Some townsfolk accused me of that the night before I left to come here. I told 'em it wasn't true. They searched the cabin and didn't find anything, but I'm not sure how long that will last before someone discovers her. And it could

189

bring trouble for Charlie and his family if she's staying with them."

"This isn't good, Chase."

"Gee, boss, I didn't realize that," he said, his voice thick with sarcasm.

"I know that, of course. You could send her back to her people."

"Just give her a horse, point her east and say, 'Adios?' " he said sarcastically. "I offered to take her, but she didn't want to go. I could offer again, but there's no assurance she'd agree to it. And even if she did, it'd be mighty dangerous for us. Cheyennes might not look favorably at a white man riding around their territory with a Cheyenne woman. They'd sure as hell figure I was keeping her captive and abusing her. Besides, I don't want to do that. Like I said, I'm in love with her."

"Take her up into the gold country and sit it out 'til things quiet down. I can afford to give you enough supplies to last quite a while."

"Might work, but I don't like that idea. Might be best, though."

"Only other thing I can think of is for you to head back east."

"With a squaw? Reckon the people in Philadelphia would be all right with that."

"Isn't there anyplace that would accept

such a thing? Some frontier place that no longer has an Indian problem?"

"None that I know of."

"I don't know what else to tell you, Chase. Whatever help you need, I'll give you. You know that. But there's not much I can do."

Tanner smiled wanly. "Maybe I could bring her here and live with you and Edna." When Harker blanched, Tanner's smile widened. "I'm joshin', Mr. Harker."

"I know that, but you had me going there for a moment. To be honest, if I could do so without endangering my family, I would not hesitate. Of course, Edna might shoot me in that case." He paused. "You plan on spending any time here?"

"Not much."

"I thought not. Would it help if I had someone else drive the wagon to Kiowa so you could ride straight to Charlie's and talk things over with him? A couple days later, you can go to town and head off on your rounds."

"Let me think on it. I'll let you know tomorrow."

"You're just full of good news, Chase, you know that?" Charlie Wilkins said. "Well, full of something anyway, and it ain't brains."

Tanner had just finished explaining the

191

situation with Elmira Cloud Dancer to Wilkins. He was confused by the half-breed's response.

"Do you really think I'd let Elmira just wander out, not give her a home? Do you?"

"No," Tanner mumbled.

"Even if I wanted to do that, Nettie'd have my scalp hangin' from her dress instead of a lodgepole like in the old days, not that the Osage used lodgepoles much."

"I don't want to endanger you and your family, Charlie."

"I'll decide who and what endangers my family. We've been endangered all our lives, practically. At first, it wasn't too bad because frontier towns were acceptin' of half-breeds and 'tame' Indians, but once more whites moved out west, well, folks like us weren't so welcome anymore. It's one of the reasons we're livin' out here."

"But . . ."

"No buts, Chase."

"Elmira can stay here as long as she wants and as long as you need her to. Me and my boys'll protect her just as fiercely as we will Nettie and Pearl and do it against red devils or white ones."

Tanner shook his head, amazed and amused. "I've heard of crazy Indians, so I figured half-breeds were only half-crazy.

Talkin' to you, I'll have to revise my thinkin' and say half-breeds are full-on crazy."

"Uh, what?"

"I'm just sayin' you're crazy, Charlie, and I'm damn glad you are. Ain't too many men'd put their family in danger to protect another man's woman when two different sides might be coming after her."

"Chase, you'd do the same for me and Nettie."

"Well, of course, but . . ." He clamped his mouth shut at Wilkins' raised eyebrow. "Right, Charlie."

CHAPTER 18

"This'll be your last trip here," Wallace Quaid said as he handed Tanner payment for the supplies.

"I do something to offend you, Wally?"

"No, no, nothin' like that. It's just I heard the Indians are plannin' to raid hereabouts. They've been raidin' the ranches and such farther out and are headin' here."

"There are no other ranches farther out except for Tyler's place, and he's only a couple miles east of you, though some miles north."

"Don't matter. I got to protect my family."

"Where'd you hear this?"

"Some riders come by the other day and told us."

"And you trust these fellas?"

"Seemed trustworthy. Looked scared, too."

"You ever think they might be trying to

scare you off so they can take over your ranch?"

"Could be, I suppose." He looked thoughtful as he grabbed the first box of goods. "Look, Mr. Tanner, I ain't the most sophisticated person, but they didn't look like or act like men who wanted to be ranchers. Maybe I'm a fool, but like I said, I have to protect my family."

"Where're you gonna go? If you're worried about Indians raidin' closer to here, headin' east wouldn't be a good idea."

"That's a fact. We'll head west, maybe to Denver; see if I can find work there. Or maybe go into the minin' areas, see if I can find a good meadow there, and start another small ranch. Ought to be able to sell cattle easily out there." He put down the box of supplies on the floor of his cabin, which was made of logs dragged from farther up the stream where there were stands of cottonwoods. "Need some money to do that, though, so maybe I'll have to stick to Denver for a spell to get some cash."

"Why don't you sell this place? That'd give you enough money, likely."

"You know anybody foolish enough to want to buy this place?"

Tanner shrugged.

They took the last two small boxes inside.

Tanner started to climb onto the wagon seat and stopped. This could be the solution to his problem. "I've been called a damn fool more times than I can count, Mr. Quaid. I'll buy the place from you."

"You will?" He looked as if an angel had just dropped down from heaven with a wagonful of cash.

"For the right price, of course. What would you be asking for it?"

It was almost a minute before Quaid could speak. He looked as if he were mentally wrestling between hopefulness and common sense. "A thousand?" he asked.

"Too much. I'll give you five hundred. That includes the cabin, furniture and all, and the cattle."

Quaid licked his lips nervously. "Well, I am eager to move on from here, but five hundred seems low. I will need money to get started up in the mountains."

"Eight hundred. Not a penny more."

The silence grew as Quaid stood considering that. "Cash?"

"Of course."

"When can you get me the money?" His nervousness was growing.

It was Tanner's turn to stand silent as he thought. Finally, he said, "A month. I'll give you fifty now to hold it; you give me a note on a deed. I need to deliver my last load of supplies and get back to Kiowa with the wagon. I'll ride on to Denver, show the land office the deed, then ride back here with the money."

"That's a mighty long time," Quaid said, worrying that he was being made a fool of.

"I know that, Mr. Quaid, but this wagon and my horse can only go so fast. Three weeks."

"Two?" Quaid asked hesitantly.

Tanner did some figuring, then decided that if he pushed it, he could make it. "Two weeks," he agreed with a nod. He held out his hand.

Quaid tentatively took it. "I'm puttin' my trust in you, Mr. Tanner."

"It won't be misplaced." He smiled. "Now, if I'm gonna be back here in two weeks, I better be moving. See you in two weeks."

Eleven days later, Tanner stopped at Charlie Wilkins' cabin. As he dismounted, Elmira Cloud Dancer burst out of the house and barreled into him, hugging him fiercely. He laughed and held her tight, noticing Nettie Wilkins grinning widely from the doorway.

"I got news," Tanner said as he and Elmira

walked, arms around each other, into the cabin.

"What?" the native women asked in unison.

"I'll wait 'til Charlie gets back."

It was not long before Wilkins entered. "Whose horse is that out there?" Then he saw Tanner. "Howdy, Chase. Thought it was yours. Been a little while."

"Too long, I think."

"Chase says he has news," Nettie said.

"Well, get supper on the table, woman," Wilkins said. "Then we can hear what he has to say. By the looks of him, it's good news." He grinned.

When Jethro and Vin came in from tending the horses, everyone sat down to supper, wondering what was going on.

Afterward, when they all had coffee, Wilkins said, "Tell it."

Tanner wasted no time. "I bought the Quaid place. With his cattle."

"Are you crazy, Chase? You don't know a damn thing about raising cattle."

"Hell, it can't be hard if you do it, Charlie." He burst out laughing.

"I'll remember that when you come beggin' me for help." Wilkins also laughed. The others joined in. "Seriously, Chase, it ain't that easy, and you don't know anything about it."

"True enough. And I will come beggin' to you for help. But with the Quaid place, Elmira and I can live together and do so in peace. Quaid's ranch is far enough out that no one will likely bother us." He grinned. "Except maybe the Cheyennes and Arapahos."

Wilkins grinned too and nodded. "Makes some kind of sense. When're you planning to do this?"

"Soon's I can get to his place. I agreed to buy it a couple weeks ago when I was making my delivery out there. I gave him fifty bucks to hold it. I had to finish one more delivery, get the wagon back to Kiowa, then ride to Denver, settle the deed, talk to Mr. Harker, and get here. First thing tomorrow, I'll head over to his place and settle up."

"How long will you give him to leave? And where'll you and Elmira stay while his family's packin' up?"

"I don't want to take Elmira there until Quaid and his family are gone. Don't need them spreading word in Denver or some other place that there's a white man living with an Indian woman out here. I'll bunk in their barn, maybe give 'em a week to get out. I'll leave Elmira here if you've got no objections, then come back when Quaid's gone."

"Sounds good — except for one thing."

"What's that?"

"You can't just leave those cattle wanderin' around loose with no one to watch over 'em while you ride here and back. No tellin' where they'll get off to. Rustlers might show up too if they've heard you bought the place and are keepin' an eye on it. You leave, and they'll pounce."

"Hadn't thought of that."

"Told you that you know nothing about ranchin'."

"That's beginning to sink in. You have any notions of what to do?"

"You could just not buy the place. Don't show up and give him the money. You'll be out fifty dollars but save yourself a heap of trouble." He grinned.

"Then I'll just have to move in here with you and Nettie, Charlie. I figure we can take over the room Orville and Pearl share." Little Pearl looked crestfallen and about to cry. Orville looked ready to whine, but a faint smile appeared when Tanner winked at him, letting him know it was a jest.

"Well, now, I best think on it for a bit." Half an hour or so later, Wilkins said, "How's about this, Chase? Vin can go with you. He can start teachin' you a little about handlin' cattle while you wait for Quaid to leave. When he does, you come back here, get Elmira, ride back to your new home, and send Vin home."

Tanner thought that over, then looked at the younger of the two oldest Wilkins sons. "What do you say, Vin?"

"Well, I don't know," the young man said slowly.

"You'll do it, boy, or I'll take a switch to you," his father said.

"No, Charlie. I won't force him, and I won't let you do so. I won't let you punish him either. We'll think of something else."

"I'll do it, Pa," Jethro said.

Both Tanner and Wilkins looked at him in surprise but then nodded. "If you're willin', I'll be glad to have you along," the visitor said. "That all right with you, Charlie?"

The half-breed looked a little disgruntled but nodded.

"Just wonderin', Vin, why don't you want to go along? I do something to make you angry?"

"No, sir, no. Nothin' like that. It's not that I don't like you. It's just . . ." He stopped, looking at his father in worry.

"Out with it, boy," Charlie said.

"Well, it's just that with Jethro bein' the

oldest, I kind of get . . ." He stopped again.

"Kind of think you're gettin' overlooked, maybe?" Tanner asked.

"I don't . . ." Wilkins began.

"I know that, Charlie, but sometimes a younger son can feel that way, even if it maybe isn't deserved. The older gets more of the easier chores, maybe, or is given more responsibility, which generally makes sense. But it can make the younger one feel like he's not in as much favor."

"That true, boy?" Wilkins asked, almost keeping the harshness out of his voice.

Vin hung his head and mumbled, "Yes."

There were a few moments of silence as everyone waited for Wilkins' response. He finally slapped his hands on the table. "Well, dammit all," he growled. "Looks like I may have to rethink things a tad. Lift your head up, boy." When Vin did, his father continued, "But you might not like it." He grinned. "You'll be workin' even harder than before. You think your brother has it easy because he's older? Well, wait 'til you take over some of his chores. You want more responsibility, you'll get it, son. You'll probably be wishin' you went with Mr. Tanner."

Jethro laughed. "Sometimes wishin' for things ain't all that good an idea, Vin."

The next morning, Tanner and Jethro

Wilkins pulled out for the almost two-day trip to the Quaid ranch.

As they rode, Jethro said tentatively, "I think you're too old for Miss Elmira."

"You do, eh?" He was wary. He had a suspicion about what the young man was thinking and didn't want to come down too hard on him. Still, he could not let Jethro think he had hope.

"Yessir. She's a fine woman, and I . . . Well . . . She . . ." He stopped, embarrassed.

"You're right, Jethro. She is a damned good woman. It's why I love her. She's damn pretty too."

Wilkins looked dejected.

Tanner clapped him on the shoulder. "You're a fine young man, Jethro, and you'll meet a fine young woman one day."

"Not out here, I won't," he groused. "Nobody's anywhere near here, makin' it awfully hard to meet a girl."

"I reckon that's true. Well, let's get this ranch business settled, and then we'll see what we can do about it. Maybe get you into Kiowa for a spell, see if we can't dig you up a suitable young woman to make you a husband."

"That'd be good, Mr. Tanner." He smiled ruefully. "You might want to whup me, but I might steal a look at Miss Elmira from time to time when she's at the house."

"Reckon I could live with that as long as that's all it is." He smiled, but Jethro could see the warning in the man's eyes.

"Yes, sir."

Wallace Quaid looked relieved when Tanner arrived, but that turned to concern when he saw Jethro, whose dark skin and high cheekbones made him think the young man was an Indian.

Tanner noticed the look and figured he knew why. "No, Mr. Quaid, Jethro here hasn't come along to cause you any trouble. And he's not an Indian if that's what you're thinking." It wasn't much of a lie; Jethro was only three-quarters Indian. "He's just along to help me with the cattle. We'll be takin' care of them while you and the family get ready to leave. Think you can do it in less than a week?" He dismounted.

"Reckon so." He licked his lips nervously and shifted from one foot to the other.

Tanner smiled. "Waitin' on your money, I bet. Well, you should. I would be too." Tanner took a pouch out of his saddlebags and handed it to the rancher. "Count it, Mr. Quaid. I'd do that first off."

CHAPTER 19

"How many head of cattle do you have, Mr. Quaid?" Tanner asked as he and Jethro joined the rancher's family — his wife, their eleven-year-old son, a daughter about eight, and a boy barely a year old — at supper.

"About a dozen."

"About?"

"You don't know much about ranchin', do you, Mr. Tanner? It's hard to keep track of 'em sometimes. Animals wander. I'm by myself mostly. My oldest is only eleven, and while he helps, it ain't like havin' someone like this young man."

"He's right, Mr. Tanner. It is sometimes hard to keep track of 'em."

Tanner nodded. "Sorry to question you, Mr. Quaid. You're right; I don't know much about ranchin'." He grinned. "Fact is, I don't know a single thing about ranchin'. That's why I brought Jethro along, so he can help me learn."

After supper, Quaid said nervously, "We don't have much room in here, but . . ."

"We'll be fine sleeping in the barn, Mr. Quaid." He looked past the man's shoulder. "A fine meal, Mrs. Quaid."

She smiled.

"I bet breakfast'll be just as good." When Tanner saw the worried looked that appeared on her face, he quickly added, "if there's enough. If not, Jethro and me will make do. We're used to it. Can't be taking food out of babies' mouths."

"You sure we'll make do?" Jethro asked as he and Tanner headed to the barn.

"How would you feel if your ma barely had enough to feed you all and two strangers come along looking to be fed too?"

Jethro grinned ruefully. "I reckon I would make do."

"Thought you'd say that. But I bet we can help a little." He took the cloth-wrapped two-pound hunk of bacon from his saddlebag and walked back to the house. Quaid opened the door, a questioning look on his face.

"Let me speak with Mrs. Quaid if I may."

"I don't . . ." Quaid stopped. "Ada, Mr. Tanner would like to speak with you." His voice shook.

"Yes?" Ada Quaid asked, eyes questioning

as she appeared in the doorway next to her husband.

"Thought this might help in some small way." He handed her the package. "Some bacon," he added as she hesitated.

"Oh, I couldn't take that from you, Mr. Tanner."

"Yes, you can. Those children can use something with a little substance to go with their porridge." He guessed at the last but figured that was their usual breakfast.

"Thank you, Mr. Tanner," she whispered as she took the package.

"No thanks needed. You can even feed some to Wally." He winked.

Ada giggled, and Tanner could hear her saying as the door closed, "He was just joshin', Wally. He . . ."

With a grin, he headed back to the barn.

In the morning, just as the sun was making its full appearance, the Quaids' oldest son, Edgar, popped into the barn. "Ma says to hurry for breakfast."

"Tell her we'll be doin' our feedin' right here."

The boy grinned. "Ma said you'd say that, and she told me to tell you that if you don't show up at the house in the next five minutes, she'll come out here and drag you in by the ear, each of you." The boy couldn't stop the laugh that bubbled up.

"Well, then, we best be getting to the house, Jethro. I don't need my ear being tugged by an angry woman."

"Me neither."

When he entered the house, Tanner said, "I hate to sound rude, ma'am, but you better have saved most of that bacon for other meals. I didn't bring it here so you could cook it all for me and Jethro."

Ada looked crestfallen. "I saved some . . ."

"Well, that's all right, I reckon."

Ada dished up the meal with some bacon for all, though she gave most of it to the visitors. The children also got some bread soaked in the bacon grease. Tanner noticed that his and Jethro's plates were the only ones with eggs on them. He also noticed that Ada was not sitting, just pretending to bustle about.

"Ada," he said quietly. When she looked at him, he said more forcefully, "Get yourself a plate and sit!"

She stood, looking terrified, and her husband seemed almost as frightened. She did not move.

"Mrs. Quaid, I told you not to give us large helpings while you and your family barely have enough to feed a mouse. Now get a plate, sit and share in our meal." Still, she hesitated. "If you don't, I'll have to tug you by the ear to a chair."

Her terrified look turned to one of shock. When she saw the small, sly smile on Tanner's face, a giggle escaped her lips. She grabbed a plate and took a place at the table.

Tanner shoved two eggs and two pieces of bacon from his plate onto hers, then gave Jethro a sharp glance. The young man pushed an egg and some bacon onto the woman's plate.

"Now, let us enjoy our meal," Tanner said before digging in.

Afterward, Tanner asked, "Why didn't you just butcher a steer, Wally?"

"Well, at first, I was holdin' on to as many as I could, hopin' to sell some of 'em as soon as I got the chance. Then when you bought the place, I didn't want you to think I was takin' one of the cattle from you."

"Damn fool," Tanner muttered. Aloud, he said, "If nothing else shows up, you'll kill one this afternoon, and we can all eat well."

They'd found ten head of cattle by the next afternoon.

"I know there's some more 'round here somewhere," Quaid said.

"If there are, Jethro and I will find 'em. I don't think you're tryin' to cheat me. Now, go on back to the cabin and help Ada pack things up."

Early in the afternoon, they jumped a deer. Both men grabbed their rifles, but Jethro was off his horse first, then he knelt, aimed, and fired. The bounding animal went down as if axed.

"Hell of a shot," Tanner said in admiration.

"Gotta be good with a rifle to keep the coyotes and wolves away from the stock." Jethro shoved his rifle away, and the two rode to the carcass. The young man carved off some meat, wrapped it in hide, and tied it to the back of his saddle.

The family and visitors ate well for the next few days, and during those days, Jethro taught Tanner what he could about ranching.

"You're about hopeless," Jethro said one afternoon as they rode back to the cabin.

"That good, eh? I didn't think I was learning anything." He laughed.

Jethro shook his head, but he laughed too.

One morning, Quaid, with Tanner and Jethro's help, loaded his farm wagon, hitched up his two workhorses, and helped his family aboard. They were gone with a wave and a shouted "Good luck" from each to the others.

"Well, it's all yours now, Mr. Tanner," Jethro said as he and his boss watched the wagon fade in the distance.

"I know." The new rancher wondered if he hadn't made a mistake, but he shook off the feeling. He had done it and now would have to make the best of it. Then he remembered that he and Elmira Cloud Dancer would be able to live together in peace here.

The next morning, he headed back to Charlie Wilkins' place. The morning after he arrived there, he and Elmira set off. He thought she looked splendid even though she wore a simple blue calico dress Nettie had made for her. She wore no bonnet, preferring to let her long silky black hair flow freely. She refused to wear white women's shoes or boots; only moccasins would do.

When they arrived, Tanner picked Elmira up and walked toward the cabin. "Put me down," she protested. "I'm not hurt. I can walk."

"It's a white-eyes custom," he said with a smile.

Inside, she grabbed him and pulled his head down to kiss him. "They have a bed?" she asked when she broke off. "Robes?"

"Bed. It's not the best, but it'll do for us."

"We use now." She grabbed his hand and

started to pull him toward the door she figured was to the bedroom.

"No, not now, Elmira."

She looked hurt. "No? You don't want me after we apart so long?"

"Yes, I want you, but Jethro probably will be here before long. I'd rather not have him walk in while we're . . ."

They settled for bringing in the food they had brought from Charlie and Nettie's and storing it.

The next day, Jethro headed home, and Tanner and Elmira baptized their new home with a lengthy session of intimacy. In the days after that, they settled into their new life together as rancher and wife. With Elmira's help, Tanner managed to keep his cattle from straying much, or worse, dying, and he kept them fed. He was a little annoyed by her help at first, thinking it was not a woman's place to do such things, but he was soon grateful, especially after she insisted there was not enough to keep her occupied at home alone all day.

Occasionally, Jethro would show up to lend a hand. Tanner didn't mind at first, but it began to irritate him. One day, just before heading out to the range, he noticed that Elmira seemed agitated. "Something worryin' you, Cloud?" he asked. While he called her Elmira most times, he liked her Cheyenne name and the way it sounded when he used it.

"It's Jethro. He . . ."

"He botherin' you?" Tanner's dander began to rise.

"No, not botherin'. Just starin' all the time."

"I'll speak to him." That day, as the two men rode out to check on the cattle, Tanner said, "I know I said I didn't mind you stealin' a glance at Elmira now and again. I didn't mean you should be starin' at her all the time. It's startin' to spook her, and if it keeps up, I'll take strong exception to it. You won't like what happens when I do."

"Hard not to, Mr. Tanner," Jethro said, hanging his head. "But I'll do my best."

"Good. And like I said, we'll see what we can do to find an appropriate woman for you."

When fall told the people it would be arriving soon, Tanner drove five head of his eleven — he had found another one weeks after Quaid left — cattle to the Wilkins place. Elmira came along and drove a small wagon, a new experience for her. He placed the animals in a temporary rope corral with eleven head of Wilkins' cattle. They drive them to Kiowa in the morning, hoping to get a decent price in the town.

That evening, after supper, as he and the half-breed sat outside the cabin enjoying the cooler weather and coffee with a small dollop of whiskey, Tanner said, "Jethro needs a wife. Probably Vin too, but certainly Jethro."

"He say something to you?" Wilkins asked, surprised.

"Not exactly, but he's been sneaking peeks at Elmira. Nothing untoward," he added when he saw his friend's shocked look. "I told him a peek now and again would be all right, but I think he's taking advantage. I don't want it to get out of hand."

"I'll speak to him first thing."

"Instead of that, it'd be better to find him a wife. I told him we'd see what we could do as soon as we could, but I don't think it's fair for the young man to wait forever. And it might lead to trouble."

"You have any ideas?" Wilkins had never given much thought to it and realized now he should have done so long ago.

"There's a few marriageable girls at one of the ranches and a farm, but I'm figurin' those folks might not be so fond of havin' a three-quarter-breed as a son-in-law."

"Not around here, they won't. That's for

"certain."

"You could take him into Kiowa and stay awhile, hoping he can latch onto some girl who'd be foolish enough to join him."

"Kind of like Nettie and Elmira," Wilkins said with a laugh.

"Yep. But there'd be the same problem there. Not too many girls are gonna want a man who's more Indian, in looks anyway, than white."

"Don't leave much in the way of options."

"Nope. But there are three I can think of, two of 'em not very good. One, take him down to Pueblo. I hear there's a lot of Mexicans and mixed bloods down there. He might not be out of place."

"What about Nettie and the cattle?"

"Leave Vin here. He and Orville should be able to keep an eye on things as long as you're not gone more than a couple months."

"The second?"

"Take him back to Nettie's people and let him find a nice Osage woman."

"Still have to leave Nettie and the cattle in Vin and Orville's care. And if I went back to talk to the Osage and didn't bring Nettie, my life would be cut short when she shoots me." He sighed. "The third?"

"Three options here too, really. Make a

quick trip back to Nettie's people — alone — or write a letter to someone you know and trust there, asking him to find a couple of suitable girls and arrange to get 'em out here. Kind of like mail-order brides."

"Doesn't give anyone much say in the matter," Wilkins said thoughtfully. "Anything else?"

"Send Jethro himself back there with the letter. Let him pick his own woman with your friend's help."

"That last makes the most sense, maybe, but it is worrisome. I'll think on it."

CHAPTER 20

Tanner and Wilkins drove their cattle into a small feedlot at the southern end of Kiowa, then rode to the livery stable, where they left their horses. The one hotel in town was a short walk, but they were not greeted kindly.

"We don't let Indians in here," the desk clerk said.

"I'm not an Indian," Tanner retorted.

"Not you. Him."

"He ain't an Indian either. Just a fella who spends too much time outside. It darkens his skin something awful."

"Like hell. Now, get out, both of you. We don't serve Indians or Indian lovers."

"No place else to stay in town."

"That's your problem."

A middle-aged couple walked in just as Tanner turned. He shook his head. "I'd find some other accommodations, sir, ma'am," he said in a conspiratorial voice. "This place

217

is crawlin' with mice and rats. Bugs, too. Every room is infested. Lice crawlin' all over every bed, cockroaches havin' revels in every corner. Disgustin'."

The couple hurried out the door.

"See you," Tanner called to the clerk over his shoulder.

The man was seething. "You wretched devil. You just cost me a paying customer. Looked pretty well off, too."

Tanner smiled unctuously. "That's your problem. Well, Charlie, we better leave. I think we should stand outside and let people know how terrible with vermin this place is."

"You wouldn't dare!"

"Sure I would."

"I'll have the law after you."

"I ain't breaking the law. Just talking to people. No laws I know of against fibbin' a little."

"All right, dammit, you can stay. Just keep out of sight. And use the servants' entrance around back to come and go."

"Reckon we can do that."

In their room, Wilkins shook his head. "We're gonna have problems wherever we go in this town, I figure. Won't be able to find a place to eat or drink or anything else, I suppose. Gonna be a tough week 'til we sell off the cattle and pull out."

"I think you're right," Tanner said with a sigh. "I had expected some, but this is looking worse than I'd thought. You mind staying in most of the time?"

"While you go out and spend your time in eateries and saloons?"

"Of course. I'm a white man, and you ain't. You know me better than that, Charlie. I'll stay here most times, too. We can play cards or something. I'll go out and bring us back food once in a while, and maybe a small bottle now and again. We can get us some fresh air by walkin' around town after dark. And maybe I can talk to the cattle agent to see if we can move the sale up a few days."

"Doesn't sound like much fun, but I reckon it'll have to do."

"Hate to say it, Charlie, but I reckon it might be best if I handle the sale of the cattle, too. Unless you want to wander over there and see if they'll treat you any better than this place."

"Think you can handle it?"

"Only with your coachin'."

"Maybe we'll wander down there tomorrow and see how I'm treated. Cattle buyers ain't too picky about sellers sometimes."

Tanner nodded. "I'll head out and get us

some food."

"Just make sure there's coffee."

Tanner was taking in the sights of the growing town when he suddenly stopped, not believing what he saw. He pushed open the business' door and stepped inside. "What in hell are you doing here, Cobb?"

Dexter Cobb looked up from his work and the blood drained from his face. "What . . . When . . ."

"I asked what you're doing here."

"Makin' and repairin' shoes," Cobb said weakly.

"I mean, what're you doing in Kiowa?"

"Moved here a couple months ago. Some of the minin' towns aren't doing so well, and with winter comin' on, me and Aaron decided to pull up stakes and move here."

"Aaron Pitts?"

"Yes. We heard Kiowa was growin', so we thought we'd try our luck here."

"Anybody else here?"

"Lieutenant Whittemore is in Denver, or at least he was last I heard. Sid Landis has been floatin' around from one place to another."

"He's not in town now?"

"Don't think so. If he is, I haven't seen him."

"Atkins?"

"He was here a few days ago, but I haven't seen him lately."

"You and Pitts planning on causing me any trouble?"

"No, sir."

Tanner believed him to an extent. He figured Cobb and Pitts were too frightened to do anything by themselves. He also figured that if Whittemore and Landis showed up, they would change their minds; of that, he was pretty certain. "Keep that frame of mind." He left. Tanner considered confronting Aaron Pitts, but he was sure he would get the same response. He moved down the street to the first restaurant he saw and picked up several ham steaks, potatoes, biscuits, and butter. It all went into a box. In another went plates, utensils, and mugs. Getting a helper from the eatery to carry the boxes, Tanner took a large pot of coffee, and the two marched to the hotel and in through the servants' entrance. Outside his room, Tanner had the boy put the boxes down. He gave him a good tip and waited 'til he was sure the helper had gone. "Open up, Charlie," Tanner said as he knocked on the door. Minutes later, the two men were enjoying a meal.

In the morning, they finished the cold

ham steaks and drank cold coffee. Then Wilkins said, "I'm goin' down to the feedlot to see what they're offerin'."

"I'll be ready in a moment."

"You ain't goin'. At least, not all the way." He grinned when Tanner gave him a quizzical look. "I want to see what they'll give a half-breed. You can stay back, and afterward, you can see what they'll give a white man."

"Sounds reasonable."

They left the dishes and cups in the room but took the coffeepot and empty boxes back to the restaurant, then headed toward the feedlot. On the way, Tanner slowed, then picked up the pace again.

"Something wrong, Chase?"

"No, but you go on ahead. I'll catch up to you later."

Wilkins gave him a questioning look, but when he got no response, he shrugged and moved on.

So did Tanner, but at a slower pace. He stopped behind a man leaning against a post, idly watching the world roll by. "Howdy, Mr. Atkins," he said.

Don Atkins stiffened.

"I think we should take a little walk."

"Why?" the gangly young man asked with a tremor in his voice.

"Need to have us a little talk."

"Got nothing to talk about."

"Oh, I think we do. Now, we're going to head down that alley over there and discuss things."

"And if I don't want to?" Atkins began to think he had the upper hand. After all, what could Tanner do to him in the open like this?

Tanner brought his knife up between Atkins' legs, lightly pressing it against the crotch of his pants. "I think you will."

"You wouldn't do something like that," Atkins said in a voice squeaky with fear.

"You sure about that?"

"The alley, you said?"

"Yep. And if you think of runnin' before we get there, I will find you and finish this." He jiggled the knife blade.

"Yessir."

In the alley, Tanner slid his knife away and slammed Atkins against the wall of a saloon. "You and the others are still spreading lies about me, even though it's been more than three years since Sand Creek. Barton has paid the price, as has Baxter. I've warned off Cobb and Pitts, and now I'm telling you to leave off sullyin' my name with hogwash."

"It ain't hogwash," Atkins said with bravado. "You are a coward and an Indian lover. If you weren't, you would've joined the rest of us in punishin' those savages."

"It ain't cowardice not to kill women and children, nor is it cowardice not to cut their bodies up."

"But they . . ."

"Yep. That's what makes 'em savages. We're supposed to be civilized. You boys weren't on that cold November day. And I'm no Indian lover." Except for one particular Indian, he added in his mind. "I sometimes think I should've killed Pitts and Cobb and might still do so since they're here in Kiowa. But I don't relish it, and I'd rather not kill them. Or you. But if I hear you spreading lies about me again, I will do to you some of what you did to those Cheyennes. Is that clear?"

"Yessir." Fright was writ large on Atkins' face.

Tanner pulled his hand away from the young man's chest. "Go, but remember what I said."

Atkins skedaddled. Moments later, Tanner walked slowly out of the alley and headed toward the feedlot. He stopped and waited in the shade of a building until Wilkins shuffled up.

"So, what're they offering a half-redskin?"

"Fifteen dollars a head, and I had to build him up from twelve."

"I take it that's not a good deal."

"For him, it's a very good deal. For me, no."

"What did you tell him?"

"Said I had a herd that I'd likely be bringin' in a few weeks. Didn't want him to know my cattle were already here."

"Good thinking. What should he be offering?"

"I ain't sure. I think we need to do some snoopin' to see if we can find what the goin' price is."

"Maybe Mort Jenkins over at Harker's store will have some idea. I'll check with him."

"Can you trust him?"

"Not sure. We'll see what he says."

"What are cattle going for here, Mort?" Tanner asked when he walked into Harker's store in Kiowa.

Jenkins looked thoughtful. "About sixteen dollars a head, I think."

Tanner was taken aback, but he thought he saw something in the store clerk's eyes. "Seems kind of low to me."

"Well, might be seventeen. Hard to tell. It changes."

"You know, Mort, I think you're full of manure," Tanner said, taking a small gamble. "I think you got yourself a deal with the buyer over at the feedlot. You give someone a figure that's low. He knows it, and that's what he pays. Then he sends a few dollars your way. He still gets beef cheap enough that he can sell high in Denver or other places."

Jenkins' eyes widened, and Tanner knew he had been right. "More like twenty-one or twenty-two."

"Thanks, Mort. I'll not have Mr. Harker check up on you to see how much you're skimming out of the till."

Jenkins blanched. "Get out."

Tanner laughed and left, heading straight for the feedlot. "Howdy, Mr. Quimby. I came to see what I could expect to get for my small herd there."

"Eighteen dollars a head," Quimby said without hesitation.

"Seems rather low."

"Well, I might be able to go nineteen if they're fat."

"They are, and they're worth twenty-four dollars a head."

"Oh, no, no. Can't do anywhere near that." He grinned unctuously, knowing there were few other places Tanner could take his cattle, especially when they were already here and penned.

"Well, I might drop it to twenty-three."

"Nineteen, and that's it," Quimby said in a hard voice. "You don't like it, go elsewhere." Again the oily smile.

"Well, you know that ain't possible, but I could spread the word in Denver next time I'm there, which'll likely be soon, that you are cheatin' us poor ranchers. Takin' food from our children's mouths, and that maybe they should go the extra few miles to Denver to sell their cattle."

Quimby glared at him. "Twenty-two," he grumbled. "Now, get out of here before I change my mind. I'll have the money tomorrow."

"Obliged."

CHAPTER 21

Tanner and Wilkins were eating a hearty if
tasteless meal in a small eatery they had
found behind the hardware store that would
serve anyone who had cash when a man
came in and announced that Cheyennes and
Arapahos had attacked the Gregson place.

"That ain't good," Wilkins said, his ner-
vousness evident on his strong bronze face.
Gregson's place was within a dozen miles of
Wilkins' ranch.

Tanner saw no reason to respond; it was
obvious. "We got our money yesterday. No
reason we can't head out now."

They had planned to stay another couple
of days and make arrangements to have supplies brought out to their ranches by Gus
MacArthur, who had replaced Tanner on
the freighting job for Jabez Harker.

"Soon's we finish here," Wilkins said. "We
can worry about supplies later. Me and Nettie have enough for a spell. You?"

"We can make do without starvin'."

The half-breed nodded. They hurried through the rest of their meal, got a few supplies, saddled up, and rode out of Kiowa within half an hour of hearing the news.

Several miles outside town, Wilkins said, "We're bein' followed."

"I thought so, but I wanted to be sure before I said anything."

"Don't know about you, Chase, but I ain't forgivin' of men followin' me maybe straight to my home and maybe to cause violence to my family."

"So, we stop 'em and discourage such a thing before it happens?"

"Yep."

"Ain't many places we can hide to wait for 'em."

"Wolf Creek ain't far. Plenty of cottonwoods to use for cover while we wait to confront those fellas."

Before long, they rode through the cottonwoods and crossed Wolf Creek, where they stopped, tied up their horses, and waited behind tree trunks. Soon, three riders came into view. "Hold there," Tanner shouted.

The three stopped. "Who's there?" one asked.

"The men you fellas been following," Tanner said.

"We ain't followin' . . ."

"You're full of dung, friend. Ain't nothin' but a few farms and ranches out this way, and you don't belong to any of 'em."

"Yes, we . . ."

"I know all the folks out here, and you ain't among 'em. Now, you're gonna get one chance to ride out of here with your lives. Take all your guns and give 'em to one of you, who'll toss 'em all in the creek. Then do the same with all your saddlebags."

"We're not gonna . . ."

Wilkins fired and hit one of the men in the shoulder. "Next one hits someone in the head," he warned.

The wounded one cursed and snapped something to a companion. That man dismounted, collected everyone's weapons, and headed for the stream.

"I better hear a splash," Tanner said.

The man dropped the guns into the stream, sending up a small spray of water. He gathered the three sets of saddlebags and dumped them too.

"Good. Now, you other two dismount." When they did, Tanner shot one of the horses.

Taking his clue, the half-breed quickly shot the other two.

"What in hell are you doin'?" one of the

men asked, eyes wide in shock and fear.

"Making sure you don't follow. Turn yourselves around and walk back to Kiowa." When they hesitated, he snapped, "Move!"

After the three men walked away, two of them helping their wounded companion, Tanner and Wilkins also left, riding hard. They arrived at the Wilkins place in the late afternoon.

Their women happily rushed out to meet them but stopped immediately, knowing something was wrong. "Come inside," Nettie said anxiously. "Elmira, food and coffee for our men."

When the two new arrivals had eaten a little, Wilkins said, "We got word in Kiowa that Gregson's place was hit by the marauders. There's been a lot of rumors, of course, so we can't be sure it's true, but I got a hunch it is this time."

"What'll you do?" Nettie asked.

"Ain't sure. Need to think on it a little, I guess. Chase?"

"Reckon we ought to make sure it's true. If it ain't, we can relax some. If it is, well, then we'll have to decide what we should do. What we can do, if anything."

"How do we . . ."

"I'll ride over there," Tanner said. He held up his hand to forestall any objection. "You need to be here to care for your family if they hit here, and I trust Elmira in your care. I can ride fast and hard and be back in a couple days."

"Long time."

"I know, Charlie, but there's not much else we can do. We can hope it was just another rumor and everything's all right."

"Where the hell is the Army?" Wilkins wondered aloud.

"I had heard a while back that they were chasin' Indians out here but couldn't catch any. Seems the warriors were always just ahead of the troops. Or surprised smaller companies of troops with superior numbers, sending them scurrying back to whatever fort was nearby."

"Figures."

"I'll need a horse. Mine's played out after our ride here."

Wilkins nodded. "Jethro, go get his tack off the mare and saddle up that big chestnut gelding. He's got stamina and some speed. Should do well."

"Right, Pa." The young man hurried out.

"Anything I can do, Pa?" Vin asked.

"Tend my horse and Chase's while your brother is gettin' the gelding ready." When the youth left, Wilkins said, "Get some vittles together for Chase's ride. Something he can eat while he's ridin', and . . ."

"I know what's needed, Charlie."

"Sorry, woman. I'm worried, is all."

"So are we all," Nettie said as she set about gathering foodstuffs and loading a buckskin sack.

In less than fifteen minutes, Tanner hugged Elmira tightly and Nettie a little less tightly. He shook the hands of the Wilkins men, then climbed into the saddle and raced off. He didn't see all the others watching him; he didn't need to since he knew they were there.

Three days later, he was back, his horse foamy from its long run and the rider sweating despite the cool fall weather. Having been watching for him, Wilkins called Nettie and Elmira, and the three were outside the cabin waiting.

"It's true," Tanner said as he slid off the horse.

"Damn!" Wilkins exclaimed.

"It was bad, too. Everyone killed and butchered. Don't know whether what they did was normal for them, or they're still payin' back for the depredations at Sand Creek. Hard to believe that, though. It's been three years."

"That Lieutenant Whittemore and some others don't seem to mind holdin' a grudge for three years."

"Reckon that's true."

"What do you figure we should do, Chase?"

"Hell if I know. I did some thinking on the way here, but I didn't come up with much of a solution. I'm too beat to think clearly now."

"You go on and take our room," Wilkins said. "Get yourself some sleep."

"Don't want to put you and Nettie out any."

"You don't argue," Nettie said. "We've slept on the floor before. We can do it now."

"She's right, Chase. Now go."

"Food first, if any's available."

"Coffee is," the Osage woman said. "Food won't be too long."

"Obliged, Nettie."

Before long, Tanner was gobbling beef-steak and turnips. As he ate, he asked, "Whare's Jethro?"

"Over at your place, keepin' an eye on your cattle."

Tanner nodded. "Soon's I get a little rest, I'll head over there and send Jethro back here."

"He can stay if you need him. Me, Vin, and Orville can keep an eye on things."

"I'll see." Tanner paused to swallow another gulp of coffee. "Like I said, I ain't sure what to do, but I'm thinking you ought to consider pullin' up stakes and movin' on."

"Ain't likely. This is our home, Chase."

"I know, Charlie, but it ain't just you and the older boys. You got Nettie to worry about, and Pearl. You don't want the females to be found by the damn Cheyennes or Arapaho." He ignored Elmira Cloud Dancer's pained expression.

"Where in hell're we gonna go? Ain't too many places acceptin' of a half-breed, his full-blood wife, and four three-quarter-breeds."

"I know. I'd suggest heading back to Nettie's people, but that means going through a heap of land full of hostiles. Maybe the Army'll start having better luck trackin' down the warriors."

"We can hope, though I don't trust the Army very much."

Tanner cast a sharp look at Wilkins, then nodded and turned back to his meal. After finishing, he headed into the Wilkins' room and collapsed on the bed. He was instantly asleep, so he was unaware that Elmira came in, sat on the edge of the bed, and gently stroked his hair. He was also unaware of the tears that dribbled slowly down her cheeks.

Tanner awoke in the morning, waking the Wilkins family as he entered the main room of the cabin. "Sorry," he mumbled.

"We needed to be up anyway," Wilkins said as his wife headed to the stove.

As Tanner sat, he asked, "Where's Elmira?"

"Outside, I reckon," Nettie said.

By the time he had finished a cup of coffee, Tanner was beginning to worry. He pushed up and went outside. She was not to be seen. His concern growing, he went to the barn and looked inside. The mare she usually rode was gone. "Damn fool," he muttered as he grabbed a saddle blanket and saddled and bridled his horse. As he finished, Wilkins walked in.

"What's going on, Chase?"

"Elmira's gone, and so's the mare."

"Ah, no. Well, hold on, I'll get Vin, and we'll go chasin' after her."

"No, Charlie. Finding her is my job."

"Might be, but with three of us, we can cover a lot more ground."

"Just keep watch on your family, Charlie. I know that horse's tracks, so maybe I can pick 'em up and follow 'em. Lord knows how much of a head start she's got, though."

"Watch yourself out there, Chase. If she's gone back to her people, it could go rough

236

on you if you're found."

"I will." They walked outside, and Tanner swung into the saddle. "See ya, Charlie." He galloped off.

Tanner wasn't the best tracker, but it was fairly easy for him to pick up her tracks since he figured she'd be heading for the Smoky Hill, which was where reports said the hardest of the Cheyenne and Arapaho warriors were living when not raiding elsewhere.

He rode fast. If she had left shortly after the Wilkins fell asleep, she roughly had an eight-hour head start. If she was pushing it, she'd covered a lot of ground in that much time, so he had a lot of ground to make up.

By mid-afternoon he was beginning to despair, thinking it might be impossible to catch up with her or that she had already found her people and he was riding to his death. Or maybe she found them and they killed her. Or maybe . . .

Then he saw her. He kicked the horse into a flat-out run even though it was tired and foamed from the ride already. Cloud Dancer must have sensed him, and she looked back over her shoulder. She got the horse moving, but the mare was also tired, while Tanner's gelding was already in motion. Tanner rode up alongside Elmira, grabbed the mare's reins, and slowed both horses until they stopped.

"Get down," he ordered.

"No."

"You know, woman, if I didn't love you, I'd knock you off that horse. Now, get down. We'll talk and let the animals rest a bit. They've been ridden hard."

She dismounted, her face tight, her body rigid with anger and worry. He slipped off his horse, took her resisting body in his arms, and stroked her hair,

"Why'd you go and run off like this?" he asked.

"I'm a damned Cheyenne and no good, like those others who attacked that farm. I'll butcher Nettie and Charlie because I'm a savage and . . ." Tears started.

Tanner recalled what he had said about damned Cheyennes and Arapahos and he shook his head, angry with himself. "You know damn well I didn't mean you when I talked about damned Cheyennes. I meant the warriors runnin' around butcherin' people. I didn't like it when white men slaughtered and cut up Cheyennes at Sand Creek, and I don't like Cheyennes killin' and hackin' up whites, either." He paused, sighing. "I wish it would stop. I wish I could make it stop, but I can't. You running back to your people won't solve anything, and it'd make me mighty lonely. And I'll tell you this, Elmira Cloud Dancer. Even if you were a damned Cheyenne, I'd still love you."

She looked up at him, fear and hope mixed in her eyes. "Really?"

"Yes'm. Now, let's head home. We'll walk the horses a while, let 'em recover some. We'll likely have to spend the night out here, and I can tend 'em then."

Elmira squeezed him. "I don't mind," she said, smiling.

CHAPTER 22

Tanner and Elmira arrived at their place just before dark two days later. Jethro Wilkins warily peeked around the barn door when he heard the noise. With a sigh of relief, he stepped outside.

"Howdy, Mr. Tanner, Miss Elmira."

"Howdy, Jethro," Tanner responded.

"Want me to tend the horses for you? I was just taking care of mine when you rode up."

"That'd be appreciated. This way, Elmira can get food started. Bet you'll be glad to eat some of her cookin' even if hastily made instead of your own." He grinned as he and the woman dismounted.

"That's a fact." He paused. "Something wrong, Mr. Tanner?"

"Gregson's place was hit by the Cheyennes a few days ago. Family murdered, and . . . well, the bodies were not left untouched."

"I didn't know 'em, but it's too bad it happened to them. Bein' mostly an Indian myself makes it all the harder to take."

"Elmira feels the same."

After Jethro took the reins of the newcomers' animals, Elmira hurried into the cabin.

"First thing tomorrow, you'll head back to your family's place," Tanner said. "Everyone was all right when we left, but with the situation the way it is, we can't be sure it hasn't changed." He noticed the conflicted look in the young man's eyes. "What is it, Jethro?"

"Well, I'd sure like to get back to my family, but are you and Miss Elmira gonna be all right here by yourselves? Back home, there's Pa and Vin. Even Orville can fight these days, now that he's grown a little, and Ma ain't no scaredy-cat. They're maybe more prepared than the two of you."

"I appreciate your concern, Jethro, but I think we'll be all right. And better you're with your folks should those devils show up."

Jethro looked relieved but worried.

"Go on and tend the horses. I'll see if Elmira needs help." She didn't, so Tanner went back to the barn and helped care for the animals. When they returned to the house, Elmira was setting plates of smoked ham and hastily boiled potatoes on the table. Moments later, mugs of coffee followed.

"Thanks, ma'am," Jethro said.

Tanner noticed that the young man still looked at Elmira with hope in his eyes, but he shrugged it off. He knew Jethro would do nothing untoward.

As they ate, Tanner said, "Your pa suggested we fort up at his place for a spell."

"Might be the smart thing."

"Might be, but I don't like leavin' my home, nor do I like to be a burden to your folks." To head off any protest, he quickly added, "I know they won't think of it that way, but I will."

"It'd be safer for everyone."

"Reckon it would, and I still might change my mind, but for now, I want to keep to my home."

They were silent for a bit, then Jethro said, "Like I told you, I could stay here, help keep an eye on things. I'm a good shot in case we are attacked."

Tanner noticed the longing glance the young man cast at Elmira. The woman was aware of it and kept her eyes averted.

"Your folks need your help too, and it's best for a man to be with his kin in times of danger."

Jethro nodded sadly.

After some thought, Tanner said, "One thing that might help is for you to take the rest of my cattle with you. Put 'em in with your father's."

"How would that help?"

"Might not, but it might be less of an incentive for them to attack here. Of course, if they're only interested in killin' white men, that won't make a difference. If they're thinking they could use the beef with the buffalo growing scarce in some places or want to cause us whites more trouble than just killin' us, having no cattle might discourage 'em."

The young man pondered that, then shook his head. "I don't think that'd discourage them at all." He offered a feeble grin. "Might give 'em more encouragement to attack our place."

"My five steers won't make that much difference," Tanner responded with his own weak grin.

"If that's the way you feel, Mr. Tanner, I'll take 'em along."

That night, as they were preparing for bed, Elmira said, "I don't like the way that young man looks at me."

"You thinking he'll harm you?"

"No. It's . . . I feel like he wants me like . . . like you do."

"He does." At her shocked look, he said, "But he won't do anything. He just looks at you because he's longing for a woman. He's lonely, and you're a mighty beautiful woman. Can't blame a young fella looking and wishing. He ever attempts to touch you, though, let him know I'll kill him. If he persists, stab him or hit him with anything handy and come get me."

"All right." She didn't seem convinced.

"Come here," he ordered gently. When she did, he took her in his arms. "I ain't about to let that young man — or any man — get between you and me. I'll gut-shoot anyone who tries to take you away from me." He paused. "Unless you ever want to leave. You ever want another man, you let me know, and I'll not stand in your way. I'll miss you something awful, but I won't stop you."

"I love you, Chase Tanner."

"And I love you, Elmira Cloud Dancer."

"Tanner!" someone bellowed.

Tanner looked out the window to see a small group of men sitting on their horses about thirty yards away. Sid Landis was at the head.

"Get my rifle, Cloud. Take yours and go into that corner." He pointed. In moments, the Spencer was in his hands. He cracked

244

the door open just enough to yell, "Get off my land!"

"You have two choices, Tanner. You and that whore of a squaw come out, or we burn the place down."

"And you have two options, Landis. Get off my land, or decide which one of you dies first."

"You ain't about to shoot one of us. That'd sign your death warrant."

"Maybe, but at least one of you, and likely more, will be dead before you can get me."

"We'll see about that." Landis and his men began moving forward and spreading out.

"Damn." Tanner opened the door a little more, stuck the barrel of the Spencer out, and fired. The bullet kicked up dirt a foot in front of Landis' horse. "Next one takes you out," he said as he levered a new cartridge home. He slammed the door shut as several men fired, the slugs thudding into the wood. He slipped toward the window and watched as a panicky Landis ordered his men to stop firing.

"Let's talk about this," Landis shouted.

"Nothing to talk about," Tanner said as he moved back to the door and cracked it open again so he could be heard. "You either get off my land or get shot."

"Let's be reasonable about —"

"You expect me to be reasonable when an armed mob shows up at my house and orders me and my wife to come out so you can shoot us down? You must've lost your reason — if you ever had any."

"We just want to talk."

"That ain't what you said at first, and if you just wanted to talk, you wouldn't have brought seven or eight men. A couple would be more than enough."

"But . . ."

"No buts, Landis. You came here to kill me and her, and if I agree to talk with you boys, you'll kill us soon's an opportunity presents itself."

Landis argued with a couple of men near him, then angrily snapped at them. He turned his face back to the cabin. "Just me and you, Tanner. We'll talk at your door."

Tanner shook his head at the man's audacity but took a few moments to think about what could be done. Finally, he sucked in a breath and slowly released it. "If you really want to talk, this is what's gonna happen. First, you will dismount and drop your pistol, rifle, and knife in that water trough over there."

"But I . . ."

"Like I said, no buts. Then, each of your men, one by one, will dismount and put their weapons in the trough, followed by their boots."

"I ain't gonna do no such thing," one of the men said.

"Shut up, Marks," Landis snapped. "If you're gonna shoot us, Tanner, go ahead and do it now. No need to kill unarmed men."

"Should've thought of that at Sand Creek. Once that's done, everyone will unsaddle his horse and pile the saddles up next to the trough."

"No!" another man said.

Tanner fired, and the bullet shattered the man's saddle horn. The rider gasped as splinters landed in the crotch of his trousers. The bullet also scraped a pant leg as it continued its flight.

"As I was saying, once that's done, the men will send their horses running. Then they will sit together where they are right now."

"This is humiliatin', Sid," Don Atkins said indignantly.

"Shut up, Don," Landis said. "Bein' humiliated is better than being dead. I figure Tanner really doesn't want to shoot any of us. I also figure he will do so if necessary."

"Smart man, Landis. You boys can start.

You first, Landis."

Grumbling and cursing, the men dropped their weapons and boots into the trough, unsaddled their horses, and sent the animals off by smacking them on the rump. Then they sat.

"All right, Landis, come on ahead. You boys best sit still. You'll be watched. Someone moves, Landis gets a bullet in the head, then I start shooting you boys."

A worried-looking and sweating Landis entered the cabin. He saw Elmira in the corner holding a pistol. "She knows how to use that thing, I reckon?"

"Yep. Be happy to, considering her feelings toward men like you." He indicated that Elmira should go to the window to watch, then said, "All right, Landis, strip."

"What?" The man was confused.

"It was a simple order."

"But . . ."

"What did I tell you about buts? Now, I am tense and unhappy. My patience is about as low as a snake's belly. It's true what you said to those boys; I really don't want to shoot anyone, but I will. Despite not wanting to shoot, I am not against causing other damage. Now, shuck your duds."

"Why?"

"To make sure you don't try anything. A

naked man is usually reluctant to cause trouble. Being the nice guy I am, I didn't want to humiliate you any more than necessary in front of the others, so I waited 'til you were in here. Now, do as you were told."

"With her watchin'?" Landis asked in a whisper.

"She's lookin' out the window."

With a sigh, knowing that Elmira was at least glancing at him, Landis did as he was told until he was naked.

"Sit," Tanner said, pointing at a chair. When the man did, Tanner asked, "Why'd you come out here to kill us?"

"We didn't . . ." The look in Tanner's eyes stopped him. "We found out you were livin' with a Cheyenne squaw."

"How?"

"That's not important. Given that, and knowin' you're an Indian lover, we came for you."

"I'm not an Indian lover except in one case." His eyes flicked to Elmira.

"You showed your true colors at Sand Creek, doin' your best to save Indians."

"I was trying to save women and kids. Peaceful people living under the protection of the U.S. Army."

Landis looked like he was going to argue but decided against it. "We thought you were an Indian lover. I still think so despite what you said, and because you were livin' with a squaw and were friends with a damn half-breed and his Indian family."

Tanner clenched his teeth as anger rippled through him at the thought that these pseudo-vigilantes knew about the Wilkins family. He looked at Elmira and could see the worry and fear in her eyes.

"Well, we thought you were collaboratin' with the Cheyennes and Arapahos, tellin' 'em where to attack."

Tanner was flabbergasted at the wildness of the man's accusations. "You're even crazier than I thought, Landis. That's such a damn-fool notion that I ain't even sure what to say to it other than it's a damn-fool notion." He paused. "That does present us with a problem."

"What's that?"

"What to do with you and the others out there."

CHAPTER 23

"If I let you and your friends out there go and you still believe such an outlandish idea, you, them, and probably a bunch of other would-be Indian-killers will come back here in a couple days and kill us. That is something I do not wish to happen, as you might well understand."

"We'll promise. I'll convince them."

"Hogwash. The manure you're spillin' is getting close to as tall as Pike's Peak." He thought for a few moments. "I could just kill you all."

Landis gasped.

"It'll likely take days before the folks of Kiowa realize you ain't coming back and come looking for you. They might find what the scavengers have left, or I could drag 'em all in here and set the place on fire. Either way, we'd have enough time to head north. New goldfields up that way, and no one to call me a coward or Indian lover." He looked thoughtful. "That's looking more and more like a fine idea."

Landis looked as if he were going to lose his last meal. "You can't," he cried out. "You'd kill seven men just because? You say you're not an Indian lover, but that would only show you were. People will hunt —"

"So," Tanner interrupted, "you see my problem. I either let you go, signing a death warrant for me and Elmira, or I slaughter a bunch of men who, while not exactly innocent, are unarmed. That too will bring us trouble. Quite the predicament."

"Kill them," Elmira said harshly. "Some, maybe all, were at Sand Creek and took part. They don't deserve to live."

"There is that, yes," Tanner acknowledged.

Landis was covered in sweat, and his fearful eyes flicked from Tanner to Cloud dancer and back. He had thought her just an Indian woman and not worthy of worry, but the look in her eyes made her seem formidable. Landis realized that she would kill him or any of the other men without compunction. He licked his lips as he fearfully awaited his fate.

Finally, Tanner nodded. "Like I've told others, I am not a man hardened to killin' in cold blood, so I would really rather not send all of you to your Maker. Still, I can't let me and Cloud be run down by a bunch of savages. So, you and your boys will get a chance to live through this."

"How?" Landis' voice trembled.

"You and your boys are gonna walk back to Kiowa. I'll be following for a spell. I know how many men there are and who they are. If I notice one fewer at any time, I will shoot one of those who are left. Since you seem to be leading this rabble, you'll be the first. I'll shoot another every few minutes until the man comes back, or I've shot all the others. You all run, spread out, and I'll run you down. On a horse, I can cover a hell of a lot more ground than you boys can on foot. I'll try not to kill anyone, but I'm not the best shot God ever put on this earth, so I might do so when I only want to wound 'em. Still, woundin' 'em will make it even harder for them to walk."

"Won't be necessary," Landis worriedly suggested.

"Hope not. Not sure how long I'll follow, but it'll be far enough that you and the others will think twice before turning around and heading back here."

"Two men edgin' toward the trough," Cloud Dancer said.

Tanner swiftly opened the door. "Tell 'em, Landis."

"Stop where you are," the ex-soldier bellowed. "Now!"

The tension mounted, then Cloud Dancer said, "They're moving again."

Tanner fired the Spencer, and the bullet plowed into the floor an inch or two from Landis' foot.

Landis screeched and almost lost control of his bladder. "Stop!" he roared.

"Did they, Cloud?"

"Yep. So far."

Tanner moved to a chest against the back wall. During his days with Harker, he had accumulated several more guns. He pulled out two more Colts and another Spencer repeater. He grabbed two boxes of shells for the rifles and three belt boxes of paper cartridges for the pistols.

Making sure all were loaded, he gave the second rifle to Cloud Dancer, hooked the hard leather boxes onto his belt, and shoved the two extra Colts into his belt, wishing he'd had the foresight to get extra holsters.

"All right, Mr. Landis, time to get dressed." As the ex-soldier hurriedly did so, his face again red as he realized Cloud Dancer peeked at him occasionally, Tanner said to his wife, "Get the horses when we're outside."

Tanner turned to Landis. "I told you

before, I'm mighty low on patience. If your men give me any difficulty at all, I'll shoot one. Understand?"

"Yes," Landis hissed, torn between fear and anger. The latter won temporarily. "I'll get you for this, Tanner. You'll regret all this."

"Outside," Tanner snapped, shoving the redressed Landis outside and telling him to walk toward his men. He kept his rifle inches away from Landis' back. Cloud Dancer hurried to the barn.

Tanner stopped Landis a few yards from his seated men. Several demanded to know what was going on, but Tanner and his hostage kept quiet. Time dragged on, but fifteen minutes later, Cloud Dancer walked two saddled horses out of the barn. She mounted one, then kept her pistol aimed at the men while Tanner swiftly swung into the saddle. "All right, boys, time to head home."

The men stood, looking confused. "Like this?" one finally asked.

"I could tie a rope around you and drag you behind the horse if that'll suit you better."

"Hell, no. I ain't walkin' anywhere without my boots," another said.

With a sigh of resignation, Tanner shot the man in the shoulder. "Now walk. You last, Landis, where I can keep an eye on you."

Frightened by this possibly crazy man, the men turned and shuffled off.

Things went fine for about an hour, but then the men started to slacken their already leisurely pace. The obvious stalling tactic annoyed Tanner even more. He moved the mare up until the animal pushed Landis in the back. "Pick up the pace," he ordered.

Landis growled but urged his men on.

It was well after dark when one of the men started drifting toward the side where Cloud Dancer was riding. With the half-moon and plenty of stars, it was easy to see. "Tell that son of a bitch to get back with the others, Landis," Tanner ordered.

"Get back here, Marks!"

The man ignored him.

With a shake of the head, Tanner fired, the bullet kicking up dirt near the man's foot. The man hesitated, then lunged at Cloud Dancer. The Cheyenne fired her Colt twice. One slug sliced a chunk out of the man's thigh, and the other sank into where the shoulder met the upper arm. Marks fell.

"A couple of your boys should go help him."

With a little hesitation, two men helped Marks up and aided him in walking back to

256

the group.

"You're already helpin' one man with a shoulder wound and now another with two bullets in him. You're only making it harder on yourselves. Start moving."

Another hour or so on, the men started to slow again, but Tanner figured it was exhaustion. The men had been walking in stocking feet for more than nine hours and were nearly played out. They came to a small stream. "All right, boys, stop."

When the men did so, Tanner said, "You can sleep, or you can keep going. Don't matter to me. But if you want to make it back to Kiowa alive, don't turn around. You do so and head back toward my place, I'll kill each and every one of you." He and Cloud Dancer whirled and galloped off.

Two miles away, the two stopped at another stream and let the horses drink. Tanner hobbled them and let them out to graze and rest some. "You all right, Cloud?"

"Yes. A little tired, but not bad. We go home now?"

"No. We head to Charlie's. What those men said leads me to believe they know about Charlie and Nettie, and I fear that almost as soon as they get back to Kiowa, they'll rest up and head out to attack the Wilkins."

257

"We warn them." It was a statement, not a question.

"Yep. Maybe get 'em to move on."

"Good. We go now."

"Animals need a little more time to recover." But within half an hour, they were back in the saddle. They made a short cold camp a couple of hours later, then pushed on, arriving at the Wilkins spread early in the afternoon.

Nettie Wilkins was surprised to see them, and her smile turned to concern when she saw their faces. "Come in, come in. Leave the horses. You look tired."

"We are, Nettie. Things've taken a turn for the worse. I need to talk to Charlie."

The Osage nodded. "Sit. I'll have food soon." She poured coffee from the ever-present pot on the stove. "Can Pearl use Elmira's mare?"

"Yeah. She's been ridden hard, but she should be all right if she ain't abused. Why?"

Nettie ignored him. "Pearl, take Miss Elmira's horse and ride out and get your father and brothers. Hurry, but don't go hard on the mare."

"Yes, Mama." The eleven-year-old ran out.

Soon food was on the table, and Tanner and Elmira ate quietly. Just after they finished, the Wilkins men hurried in. "You

258

two all right?" Wilkins asked.

"Yeah. Just tired. Got things to discuss, though."

Wilkins nodded. "Vin, you and Orville go and take care of the horses."

"But Pa . . ." Vin started.

"Go on and do as I say, boy."

The young man and the teenager left. Wilkins and Jethro sat, nodding thanks for the plates of food and cups of coffee Nettie placed before them. "So, what's brought you here, Chase?"

"Group of boys from Kiowa paid us a visit. They were led by Sid Landis. The others I smacked around at Sand Creek were along."

"I take it they were not there to help you celebrate you as their favorite rancher," Wilkins said dryly.

"That would be an accurate assessment. Claimed they wanted to talk to me, but they were really there to kill us. I discouraged them from that idea and did actually talk to Landis. They seemed to think that since I'm an 'Indian lover' livin' with a Cheyenne woman, we were colludin' with the Cheyennes and Arapahos in their attacks."

"I could see how they might think that since they're all damn fools with the brains of cow manure. What'd you do?"

"Made 'em dump their boots and weapons in the water trough. Had them pile their saddles next to it and sent their horses packin'. Walked 'em almost halfway back to Kiowa and warned 'em off."

"Think it'll take?"

"Don't know, but I have my doubts. But that's not all. They know about you and your family. I don't know how they found out. Hell, I don't know how they found out about Elmira."

"The Lord and evil men work in mysterious ways. This ain't good, though I ain't really surprised."

"If they came for me, they'll damn sure come for you."

"I know. But you drove 'em off by yourself. Me and the boys can run 'em off easier."

"Don't be foolish, Charlie. There was only seven of 'em come for us, and they weren't expecting trouble. They'll send more after you, and they won't be caught unawares."

"Not much we can do but wait it out and see what they'll do."

"You could always head to the New Mexico Territory. There ain't many Indian problems there. The Navajos are gone, the Comanches are up here or off to the east in

260

Texas, and even the Utes are mostly subdued."

"But the Americans are still there, and so are the Mexicans, neither of which favor Indians of any kind except maybe reservation ones."

"Those folks in Kiowa, as well as the other ranchers and farmers out here, might get the governor to form another militia. Even if not, a bunch of 'em could show up here, ready to kill anyone they think might even be part-Indian."

"I have no trouble killin' a passel of white men come to do me and my family harm."

"You kill the first bunch, they'll send more."

"I'll kill them, too."

"You couldn't keep that up, Charlie. Maybe instead of the New Mexico Territory, go back to Nettie's people like I suggested before."

"And like I told you before, this is our home, and we'll defend it from any attackers, red, white, or brown."

Tanner had to try once more. "You're gonna have to make a choice about the cattle and your home."

Wilkins gave Tanner a questioning look.

"If you send a couple of the boys out to watch the cattle and you and one of the others stay here, you split your forces. Be easy for those bastards to attack those out with the cattle while another bunch hits here. You can't leave Nettie and Pearl alone while all the men are out working the cattle, and if you want to stay here and continue ranchin', you can't keep everyone at the house and let the cattle run loose. Either way, you don't know how long you have before they show up. Could be in a couple days, may not be for a couple months. You can't keep up that kind of vigilance forever."

"Options don't look good."

"No, they don't."

Chapter 24

"What're you plannin' to do, Chase?" Wilkins asked.

"Ain't sure yet. I did a little thinking on it on the ride here but didn't make any decision, of course. Might go to Montana Territory. I heard there's new gold finds up there. Don't know if there's any Indian troubles up that way."

"Bein' a Lakota, I can tell you that there are plenty of Crows up there, and they ain't friendly toward Cheyennes. They are fairly friendly to whites. How they'd react to a white man with a Cheyenne woman, I ain't sure."

"Couldn't be much worse than here."

"You can't be sure of that."

"True." He paused. "The only other idea I had is a crazy one: go out to find the Cheyennes and try to talk 'em into leaving this part of the country alone."

"That ain't crazy, Chase," Wilkins said as

his wife gasped. "That's full-out insane. What makes you even entertain the notion that the Cheyennes and Arapahos would even talk to you, let alone agree to raid elsewhere instead of here?"

"Well, not me so much as Elmira."

Wilkins laughed. "What makes you think a bunch of Dog soldiers, the elite of the elite of the Cheyenne warriors, will listen to a woman any more than a white man?"

"I listen to Elmira."

"That's hogwash, but even if you did, you aren't a Cheyenne Dog Soldier."

Tanner sat there thinking, then said, "You could come with us, Charlie."

"What?" Wilkins was surprised and confused.

"You said when I brought Elmira here for the first time that you were a Lakota and that the Lakota and Cheyennes were friends, allies. I have a Cheyenne woman and a Lakota . . ."

"Half-Lakota."

"Half-Lakota along, they might listen to a crazy white man."

"Now, that almost makes sense," Wilkins said after some thought. "But I don't think it'll work. Besides, I'd have to leave my family alone, and that I won't do. Not without any kind of guarantee that doin' what you're thinkin' would work."

"But if —" Tanner cut off what he was planning to retort and instead said, "You're right, Charlie. I couldn't ask that of you, but I can't think of anything else to do. We got Cheyennes and Arapahos on one side and angry farmers, ranchers, and their townsfolk friends on the other. Me and you are stuck in between. Neither side likes us or trusts us, and we can't trust either of them."

"Puts us in a bind, don't it?"

"Yep. And nowhere to turn."

"I reckon me and the family will just hunker down where we are and hope neither side comes against us. You?"

"Don't know. All I can think of is finding the Cheyennes and try to talk 'em into leaving us alone. Damn-fool notion, I know. I suppose I'll think on it some."

"Findin' 'em will be near impossible, and if you do, talkin' 'em into not attackin' here is more than impossible."

"Hard to be more than impossible."

"Keep that to mind, Chase," Wilkins said. He swallowed some coffee. "You and Elmira are certainly welcome to fort up with us here for a spell."

"Kind of cramped in here."

"Jethro and Vin can sleep in the barn." He

glared at the two young men to stave off any argument.

"That might be best, I reckon." Tanner sighed. "Doesn't set well with me to impose on friends." Before Wilkins could respond, he said, "I know you don't see it that way, but I do. Still, it's a hell of a lot better than trying to find and talk to a bunch of Cheyenne Dog soldiers."

"Much better, especially since the chances of an attack here are fairly small. All the places the warriors have attacked anywhere near here have been on the fringes of the area."

Tanner nodded. "I'll sleep on it, but I reckon you might be right."

"Still don't know what I'll do, Charlie," Tanner said in the morning. Reckon I'll ride to our place and get some things before coming back. Give me time to think. I just wish those damned Indians hadn't started raiding around here. It's . . ."

"What'd you say?"

"I said . . ."

"I know what you said, dammit, and I'm tired of white men blamin' all the troubles around here on the damned Indians. If it weren't for Sand Creek, they likely wouldn't be raidin' in these parts."

"I suppose you're right, Charlie. Don't matter any now, though," Tanner said tightly. He pushed himself up from the table. "Get our things, Elmira."

"But . . ."

"We're leavin'."

"But . . ."

"Don't sass me, woman. It's plain that we're not wanted here. At least, I ain't. They might accept you since you're an Indian, but I ain't. I want you to go with me. You don't want to, that's your choice.

"I'll not be happy, but I'll accept your choice if you do stay here. Maybe you feel safer here or more comfortable. Doesn't matter why you want to stay if you do. I'm going out to saddle the horses. You want to come with me, meet me in the barn in a few minutes. You're not out there in fifteen minutes, I'm ridin' off." Tanner stalked out.

Elmira entered the barn as he finished saddling the mare she used. The woman was crying.

"I know this don't sit well with you, Cloud. It doesn't sit well with me either. Like I said, you want to say here and they'll have you, go ahead. You can have the ranch as soon as I leave, which won't be long. I doubt anyone will let you keep it, though, as soon as the news gets out that a Cheyenne is the owner. Maybe sell it to Charlie. Maybe he can help you get back to your people."

"No. I'm going with you. I'll miss Nettie, but my place is with you."

"You sure?"

"Yes."

"Then let's ride."

The cabin was still smoldering when Tanner and Cloud Dancer rode up. There was little left but a pile of ash with a few unburned logs scattered in the rubble. The barn, made mostly of sod, was still standing, though attempts had been made to tear it down, and the wagon had been burned. The mule, which he had let loose when he'd headed to the Wilkins' place, was nowhere to be found. Tanner hoped the animal was roaming free instead of having been killed by marauders, white or red.

"Damn Indians," Cloud Dancer spat.

"Damn white-eyes," Tanner corrected her.

"You sure?"

"Yep. Various signs tell the story, or at least enough of the story to tell it was white men."

"What'll we do?"

"For now, try to rustle up some food. Don't know where, though."

"Maybe they missed the smoked meat in the barn?" Despite the seriousness of all this, she giggled at the thought of smoked meat still being stored in the building that had not been burned.

"I think it's all gone, but I'll check. You should be able to find enough wood that can be used for a fire. We have some coffee left, so we'll at least have that."

He found a small shank of venison he had cured a few months ago and brought it out. "We're in luck, Cloud," he said as he handed it to her.

She nodded as she got the fire going. Once that was done, she sliced off a few pieces of meat and tossed them into a frying pan to heat up. Fixing coffee came next.

While their meal was cooking, Tanner took the horses to the barn and tended them, then came back and sat near the fire. He and Cloud Dancer ate in silence.

Afterward, the Cheyenne asked, "Why do you think Charlie acted that way?"

"No idea. Never expected that from him. He can be hotheaded at times, but this was unusual — hell, more than unusual — for him." He sighed. "Reckon it don't matter much anymore. We're on our own now, Cloud, just me and you."

"I don't mind."

"That may be, but I reckon it'd be best if we got you back to your people."

"I said no before, and I ain't changed my mind."

"But . . ."

"If you want me to be safe, I stay with you. Like you and Charlie talked about, we're caught between the whites and the warriors. I've seen enough of white men to know how cruel they can be. I grew up Cheyenne, and I know how cruel they can be. If I go back, men like those who did this" — she waved an arm at the remains of the house — "might catch up to us. Or the Army. I'm afraid the Dog soldiers can't hold off the Army forever. And the warriors won't quit."

"I wish they would."

"Would you give up your home and way of life because the Cheyennes and Arapahos said you must?"

"Well, no, but . . ."

"And with so many settlers moving along the trails, the railroad comin', and hunters, the buffalo are bein' killed off. As that gets worse, people will starve. I don't want to face that, so I'm not goin'. Unless you don't want me no more." She gave him a questioning look, fear in her eyes.

"Don't ever doubt that, Cloud."

"Then I stay with you. Maybe we move someplace else where there's no trouble between people like me and people like you."

"Ain't likely to find such a place."

"Then we go where there's no people."

"Wouldn't be much of a life."

"You got me, I got you. I don't need more. Maybe you do. If true, you go into a town sometimes, get drunk and foolish, then come back to me."

"You got an answer for everything, don't you, woman?"

"Women always do." She grinned.

"You got an answer for this?" He stood, pulled her up, and kissed her hard.

"Yes." She started to unbuckle his gun belt.

Vin Wilkins rode up late the next morning. Tanner watched him approach and waited with a hand on the butt of his Colt. When the young man stopped, Tanner asked, "What do you want here, boy?"

Wilkins was taken aback, but he hadn't expected a friendly greeting. He looked around, wide-eyed. "What happened here, Mr. Tanner?

"What in hell does it look like? Somebody burned us out. You can tell your father it was white men who did it, not damn Indians if that'll make him feel any better. Now, what are you doing here?"

"My folks are worried about you and wanted me to check to make sure you're all right."

"You folks don't give a good goddamn about us. That was made clear the other day."

"Pa cares, but he . . ." Seeing the look in Tanner's eyes, he said, "Maybe he doesn't, but Ma cares. You know she does. Especially about Miss Elmira."

"She send you?"

"Yessir."

"Your father know?"

"Nope. Ma told him I was goin' huntin' southwest of the ranch."

"Your pa's gonna whup your behind something awful when you get back."

Wilkins looked a little sick but nodded. "I know."

"Why didn't you tell your mother this was a fool's errand?"

"There ain't no arguin' with Ma when she gets that look in her eye. It was either do what she said and face a whuppin' from Pa or refuse to go and have her givin' me that stare she has that makes a boy — a man — feel like the bottom of a snake's belly. I figure the whuppin' won't be as bad as the other."

Much of Tanner's anger at the young man had faded, and he grinned. "Maybe you should just keep riding."

"Could do that," Wilkins said with his own grin. "But I'd miss 'em both. The others, too."

"Must be nice having a close family like that. Well, come on and have something to eat. We ain't got much, but you can share what we have."

CHAPTER 25

"Looks like the Cheyennes have been through here," Sergeant Miles Ralston said, nodding at where Tanner's house had been. He and three other men stopped in front of Tanner.

"Not Cheyennes. Whites."

"Oh, hogwash," one of the other men said.

"What're you doin' here, Sarge?" Tanner asked, ignoring the soldier.

"I haven't been a sergeant in a while. It's just Miles."

Tanner nodded.

"We're chasin' after Landis' bunch, who left Kiowa the other day. Damn fools plan to punish the Cheyennes and Arapahos."

"Good way to visit their Maker."

"Yep."

"So, why are you followin' 'em? Plan to join 'em?"

"I ain't that foolish. No, folks in Kiowa — at least those with more sense than the ones

274

who left — want to stop that gang of lunatics from finding the Indians."

"Why?" Tanner asked.

"Well, the likelihood of them finding the Indians is pretty small, though there's a good chance the Indians will find them. And it's probably impossible for those boys to punish the Indians even if they do find some warriors, but folks in Kiowa, as well as a few of the ranchers, are worried that an attack by those fellas will anger the Indians worse. That could lead to even more attacks against us."

"Maybe the Army will find 'em first. Either of 'em."

"Ain't likely. Why don't you come with us, Chase?"

"No, Miles. I got other plans."

"What're you plannin'?"

"Head north, maybe to Montana Territory. Get away from all the troubles here."

"I'm surprised you aren't stayin' here," the man who had spoken earlier said. "Indian lover that you are, there's plenty hereabouts." Seeing Tanner's flash of anger, he smiled unctuously. "Ah, yes, I've heard about you."

Before Tanner could say or do anything, Ralston pulled his horse close to the man's and punched him in the face, almost knocking him off the animal. "Did you say some-thing, Hayward?" Ralston looked at Tanner. "Mr. Hayward is an ass, Chase, in case you were wondering."

"I was thinking worse, but I'll settle for that."

"It might be good, though, if you did come with us, Chase."

"Why's that?"

"I figure it was Landis' men who did this," Ralston said, waving his hand at the rubble. "We catch up to 'em, you might get a little revenge."

"That might be a good thing."

"By the way, the others beside Carl Hay-ward with me are Barney Downing and Paul Hooper."

Tanner tipped his hat at both, a gesture that was returned.

"So, what'll it be?"

Tanner thought it over for a minute, then nodded. "I'll go saddle our horses."

"Horses?" Hayward sneered. "Come on, Miles, we're not takin' along some Indian whore, are we?"

Ralston punched him again, this time knocking him off his horse. "I suggest you keep your mouth shut from now on." He looked at Tanner. "Have at him if you're of a mind to."

Tanner took a step, then stopped. "Another time, maybe." He headed for the barn, where Cloud Dancer was hiding and watching.

Inside, he told the woman they were going with Ralston and the others and why. When he saw fear sweep into her eyes, he said, "You don't have to come if you don't want to. I can take you to Nettie's and catch up with these boys."

She looked conflicted.

"These boys won't hurt you. I'll make sure of that."

"Yes?"

"Yes."

"I come, then."

Ten minutes later, the mounted Tanner and Cloud Dancer joined Ralston's men, who had been letting their horses drink from the trough. Tanner introduced the men. "Boys, this is Elmira Cloud Dancer. You may call her Miss Elmira or Cloud Dancer; either is fine."

Ralston smiled as he greeted the Cheyenne. Downing and Hooper looked dubious but politely offered a welcome. Hayward looked scornful. "Miss Elmira?" He snorted in derision.

Tanner rode up beside his horse so they were face to face. "If you so much as insult my wife, let alone touch her, Mr. Hayward, I will kill you. I will not hesitate. I will not give you a second chance. I will not accept any apology you might try to make. Is that understood?"

"Mr. Ralston will never let that happen."

"Mr. Ralston," the former sergeant said dryly, "will be glad to shoot you should Mr. Tanner miss, which isn't likely. The same goes for you others. Now, let's ride."

Tanner and Cloud Dancer took the lead, along with Ralston, following the mass of tracks the raiders had left. Tanner was uncomfortable having the other three men, especially Hayward, behind him, but he didn't think any of them would try anything brazen. Downing and Hooper each held the rope of a pack mule; Hayward held the rope of an extra horse.

As they rode, Tanner asked Ralston, "Why are you doing this, Miles?"

"Told you, we're tryin' to prevent more trouble."

"That's what you're doing, not why you're doing it."

"Ain't exactly sure why. I spent most of the last few years tryin' my luck in the goldfields, and when that didn't pan out," — he grinned at the pun — "I worked for an undertaker, buildin' coffins. Needed a lot of 'em, unfortunately, between the weather, a few Ute raids, mine accidents, men fallin' over cliffs, gunfights, and a heap of other reasons. Finally got tired of that, though, and wound up in Denver. Took a job as a guard for a load of supplies for a store in Kiowa for a fella named Jabez Harker."

"Worked for him for a number of years 'til recent, when I purchased the place here."

"Seemed a decent fella."

"He was . . . is. Treated me well despite all the rumors and such."

"They been followin' you all this time?"

"Yep. Don't know why exactly. Baxter told me Whittemore hated Indians for having killed and butchered a bunch of his family members."

"Can't blame him for that, I suppose."

"Reckon not. Barton also said Whittemore hated me in particular for wallopin' those boys of his back then. Instead of just tryin' to kill me, though some folks did take a couple shots at me in the dark, he wanted me to suffer in my shame."

"What ever happened to Barton? I ain't heard of him. Some of the folks, mainly Aaron Pitts and Dexter Cobb, said he disappeared."

"Reckon you could say he did."

Ralston looked at him in question but realized he should leave it alone.

"You never did answer me as to why you're doing this."

"Town fathers in Kiowa were worried about Landis leadin' a bunch of men on their quest to punish the Indians. Thought it was a fool's errand, as did anyone with sense. They were lookin' to put together a small group to try to run 'em down and convince 'em to give up this foolishness. They knew I was former Army and had been a guard on the supply wagon, so they approached me."

"And you said yes?" Tanner was surprised.

"Not at first. Then they showed me the sack of gold coins. Changed my mind." He grinned.

"You're risking your neck for a sack of gold?"

"You ain't one to point fingers, Chase. From what I hear, you risked your neck takin' wagons east and back. Twice! All for a couple sacks of gold."

"Reckon you ain't the only damn fool then, are you?"

"Nope"

"How'd that horse's ass Hayward come to be with you? I can't figure you'd want to have such a fella along."

"He thinks he's good with a gun, and he thinks he'd like to kill Indians like his brother Garrett, who's with Landis."

"Don't seem like good reasons for you to take him along."

"He's also the brother of Rich Hayward."

"Who's he?"

"The fella who put up most of the coins in that sack of gold."

"That would do it, I reckon."

A couple of hours later, Tanner asked, "Can I trust you to keep an eye on Cloud, Miles?"

"You can. Why?"

"Despite those mule loads of supplies, some fresh meat'd be good if I can scare something up."

"That'd be good, but it looks pretty barren out here."

"Might be."

"Paul, move the supplies from one mule to the other. Take that one with you, Chase."

Tanner nodded. Minutes later, he took the mule's rope. "It'll be dark before long. Comanche Creek's only a few miles ahead. Plenty of wood and water. Good place to camp. I'll meet you there." He paused. "I'm counting on you, Miles."

"I know. Good huntin'."

There was still a little light left when Tanner rode into the camp, an antelope carcass hanging over the mule's back. He stopped, eyes blazing when he saw Hayward tied to a tree, splay-legged. "What happened?" he demanded of Ralston.

"He insulted Miss Elmira. Nothing more."

"I told him — and you — what I'd do for even an insult." He started toward Hayward, but Ralston grabbed his arm.

"Don't, Chase. He ain't worth it. I'll keep him trussed up from now on."

Tanner stood there fuming, then nodded tightly. "Those boys know how to butcher a pronghorn?"

"Doubt it."

"Cloud?" He chucked his chin at the animal.

The woman nodded, hauled the carcass off, and dragged it to a tree. Tanner took the animals to be tended. When he finished, he walked up to Hayward and kicked him square in the privates.

Hayward blanched and almost passed out.

"You're only alive because of Mr. Ralston's benevolence. I still might ignore his request for your continued existence." He walked away to where Cloud Dancer was finishing carving off some antelope meat. He handed a chunk to Ralston. "I don't mean to be unfriendly, but you and the others'll have to make your own mess."

"Figured. I got Downing out gatherin' wood." He paused. "You asked me before if you could trust me. Now I have to ask you — can I trust you not to kill Hayward?"

"For now," Tanner said tightly.

After eating, Cloud Dancer went to Hayward's side and knelt there. She had her knife and a whetstone in her hands. She began sharpening her blade slowly, staring at the man as she did.

"Some Cheyennes bad," she said quietly but forcefully. "Some Cheyennes good. Some white men bad. Some good. My Chase is good. Mr. Ralston, he is good man, too. I don't know about other two, but you, you are a bad white man. Sometimes bad things happen to bad men so they not bad anymore. Sometimes things happen to bad men so they are not a man anymore."

She grinned almost pleasantly at the terror that had jumped into Hayward's eyes. She did not see the reactions of Downing and Hooper, though she could hear their short gasps of worry. She did not see the harsh grins on the faces of Ralston and Tanner, but she could guess at their responses. With a last swipe of the blade against the stone, she stood and walked back to her fire.

Carl Hayward almost passed out as his squashed testicles hit the hard saddle when Ralston helped hoist him onto his horse in the morning. "I need to tie you on?" the former sergeant asked lightly.

"No," Hayward managed to gargle.

"Let's go, then." Minutes later, they splashed across the creek and began following the trail again.

At dusk, they reached Rattlesnake Creek. Tanner prowled around as the others were making camp. "They camped here two nights ago, maybe three, but two for sure."

"We're catchin' up?" Ralston asked hopefully.

"Would seem that way."

With renewed spirits, they pulled out early the next morning, but they hadn't gone far when Tanner stopped, looking perplexed.

"What is it?" Ralston asked.

"Something ain't right. Stay here." He rode out a little way, stopped again, then turned more to the north and rode another few hundred yards. He trotted back to the group.

"They split up. Most of 'em kept going

the way they had been. A smaller group headed north."

"Why would they do something like that? Could they have somehow learned that Indians were raidin' up there?"

"Doubt it, or they wouldn't have split up." A worry that had been tickling his mind solidified. "Charlie's place!" he snapped, concern gripping him.

CHAPTER 26

It didn't take Tanner long to decide. "Keep on followin' the trail, Miles."

"Where're you goin'?" Ralston asked, surprised.

"That way," Tanner said, pointing at the trail that veered off. "Friend of mine lives out there, and I figure this bunch is heading there."

"Why? lookin' for more help?"

"Friend's a half-breed. I think the main group is headed to Bruckner's ranch if it's where you say it is. Don't know what the fools are planning from there, but I reckon that's where they're headed for now. Luck to you." Without waiting for a response, Tanner turned his horse and dashed off, with Cloud Dancer right behind him.

As he rode, Tanner feared what he would find at Charlie Wilkins' place. It looked like only five or six men had broken off from the main group. The Wilkins family could easily stand them off unless Charlie and his sons were off looking after the cattle.

Tanner and Cloud Dancer rode through the night, slackening the pace after the first couple of hours and stopping for only a very few hours to let the horses breathe and drink. The couple gnawed on jerky, then they got back in the saddle again.

About mid-morning, Tanner and Cloud Dancer galloped into the yard of the Wilkins place. Tanner was off his horse first, yelling, "Charlie! Nettie!" as he ran for the door.

The portal opened. Nettie barely made it out of the way before Tanner, then Cloud Dancer had barged in.

"Nettie, Charlie, are you all right?"

It was only instinct that made Tanner brace for Wilkins when the half-breed charged at him, slamming him against the wall. Tanner blocked the punch Wilkins threw at him but was not quite as successful with the one from Jethro. Then he began fighting without thought, swinging, kicking, elbowing, and grunting when punches landed on him. He was barely aware of Nettie and Cloud Dancer screaming at them to stop.

Suddenly, a loud explosion split the air, and everyone froze. It took some moments before all eyes came to rest on Nettie, who stood with a smoking shotgun in her hands. "That's enough!" she snapped. "Now, all men sit down at the table. Elmira, get coffee."

"I ain't sittin' with that son of a bitch," Charlie Wilkins spat. "Not when he's come back to finish off what his friends started."

"What the hell are you talkin' about, Charlie?" Tanner asked, confused.

"You know danged well what I'm talkin' about, you treacherous son of a . . ."

"Stop!" Nettie screamed. "Charlie Wilkins, does it look like this man and woman came ridin' up to try to cause trouble?"

"Well . . ."

"Don't 'well' me, husband. You know that's a foolish notion. Him and Elmira come to see how we were doin'. Maybe he heard there was trouble here."

Tanner nodded. "Me and some others were following a mob looking to kill Indians and . . ."

"And you were gonna join 'em."

"And they split up. Most were still heading east, but some were heading this way. Soon's I saw that I came here to see if you were all right. I figured I'd be too late to help since those boys had a three- or four-day head start. I also figured that since there was only four of 'em, maybe five, you could hold 'em off. But I had to check."

"You were hopin' to catch us by surprise and finish us off, weren't you?" Jethro demanded.

Tanner looked at him with disgust. "Are you taking lessons in being stupid from your father? I don't know as if I've ever come across such a thick-headed bunch of . . ."

"Indians?" Wilkins snapped.

"Horse's asses. Damn, Charlie, use your head. I suppose Vin told you what happened to my place. Whites did it, and I told him so. Next day, some fellas come by. One of 'em was a sergeant at Sand Creek in one of the two companies that didn't take part in the slaughter. He and the others said they were chasing the mob to try to stop 'em from causing more trouble with the Cheyennes and Arapahos. I joined up with 'em to see if I could help, but also to find the sons a bitches who burned my house down and kill 'em."

"You wouldn't kill your own kind," Jethro said.

"You're getting stupider by the minute, boy. I was branded a coward and an Indian lover because I wouldn't kill Indians at Sand Creek. Now you tell me I won't kill white men. Either I truly am a coward and won't kill anyone, or I can — and will — kill anyone who crosses me. Take your pick."

The silence grew as everyone glanced from one person to the others. No one had sat, and Elmira stood with her hand on the handle of the coffeepot on the stove.

Finally, Tanner said, "The last time I was here, Charlie, you questioned my friendship and accused me of being just another white man out to get Indians. Now you're flat-out calling me an enemy. I left angry that day, but I put that out of my mind when I thought you and your family might've been hurt by those scum. Unless you plan to shoot me in the back, I'm leaving here again, this time sad that I've lost a good friend. Well, someone I thought was a good friend. And I'll have to comfort Elmira since she feels the loss of her best, maybe only, friend in this world except for me." He paused to see if there was any response. There was none. "I won't be back, Charlie. You can spend the rest of your days congratulating yourself for having shed a damned white-eyed skunk, for being a proud warrior. I'll spend the rest of my days missing a man — no, a family — that I had called friends. Oh, and you can keep the cattle. Come on, Cloud. Goodbye, Nettie."

"You wait," Nettie said sternly. "I pack

some things."

"You don't need to pack anything for us, Nettie. Elmira and I will be fine."

"No, I pack for me."

For some seconds, the silence could not have been broken by a keg of dynamite. Then Wilkins said with a short bit of laughter, "That was a good one, woman. For a moment there, I thought you were leaving."

"I am." At Wilkins' shocked looked, she said, "I've had enough, Charlie. Enough of your hardheadedness, of your foolishness. Twice before you had words with Chase and once made him leave in anger, yet he came back both those times. He's helped you, taken to the older boys like they were his own. He's been good to Orville and to Pearl. He treats me — all of us — with respect, sometimes more than you do."

"Dammit, Nettie, I . . ."

"You are, like I said, a hardheaded old cuss."

"I see some tears there, woman." Wilkins had a note of victory in his voice. It quickly disappeared.

"Yes, they are there, and there'll be many more for a long time. I don't do this because I don't love you or the children anymore, but I'm determined that I won't live like this any longer. I will go with Chase and

Elmira wherever they go. I will miss you a lot and the children more, but I will be with friends instead of a hardheaded husband and children who do not care."

She set the shotgun gently on the table and turned to go to the room she had shared with Wilkins since the day the house was built.

"Stop right there, woman!" Wilkins snapped.

Nettie looked at him. "I learned English from you and many others after I left the missionaries. I listen when men talk, and I learn things. I learned words women are not supposed to say, but sometimes they are good words. So I say to you, 'Go to hell, Charlie Wilkins.'" She resumed her progress.

Wilkins looked confused, perplexed about what to do. Tanner saw it. He realized the half-breed was a proud man, and to be seen pleading with his woman in front of others would be humiliating. "Come on, Cloud," he said quietly

Nettie looked at him in panic. He smiled. "We're just gonna wait outside. Take as long as you need. He or the boys try to abuse you, yell and I'll come running. And gunning."

■ ■ ■ ■

The wait was long and nerve-wracking. After half an eternity, Nettie opened the door. She still had tears in her eyes, but the determined look was also there. "I stay," she said. "Thank you for bein' willin' to take a cranky old Osage woman with you."

"It would have been no burden, Nettie. I wish you a good life, even if it is with a hardheaded old cuss." He smiled.

With tears in her own eyes, Cloud Dancer hugged the older woman. They whispered a few things to each other, then separated.

"Before you go, Chase, Charlie said he wants you to know . . ."

"If Charlie has something to say to me, tell him to get his ass out here and tell it to me, not be a weakling and have his wife do it for him."

Nettie grinned through the tears. "I tell him."

Moments later, a conflicted Wilkins came out. Tanner told Cloud Dancer to go inside.

"Look, Chase, I . . ." The half-breed hesitated. "This is hard for me. I'm a proud man and . . ."

"I know you are, Charlie. So am I, and most any other time, I'd not need to hear

293

what I think you're gonna say. But this time, I need to hear it. Not to belittle you, but so I know you mean it. If you can't say the words, then it doesn't mean a damn thing."

Wilkins was silent for a few moments, then his spine stiffened, and he looked Tanner square in the face. "You're right, Chase. I've been a damned fool who treated a good man, a friend, like he was lower than the barn floor. And I am damned ashamed of it. This is hard for me to say."

"I know."

"Shut up. I've always thought of myself as a man with strength and the stones to stand up for what's right. I apologize, Chase. I don't know if you'll forgive me now or ever, but I swear to you as a man, as man to man, I mean that."

"I forgave you twice before, Charlie, but you abused that. This is the last time. You go back on your word this time, and I'll leave for sure. And take Elmira with me, and Nettie if she wants to go."

Wilks started to retort, then stopped. He nodded and held out his hand.

Tanner hesitated, then shook it. "Send Elmira out here. We need to get back on the trail."

"What you two need is food and rest, and what your horses need is hay, water, and rest. Come on back inside."

As they took their first steps, Wilkins looked at Tanner and offered a sly grin. "Ya know, Chase, if you ever did take Nettie with you, you might regret it. She's a hardheaded old cuss too."

Tanner chuckled. "I'll make sure I tell her you said that."

"Don't you dare!" He was appalled for two seconds before he realized Tanner was joking. He chuckled too.

After the humans and horses had been fed and had rested, Tanner and Cloud Dancer climbed into their saddles. For the tenth time in the last hour, Nettie said, "Stay here, Elmira. You'll be safe."

"No. I belong with Chase."

"Besides," Tanner said, "if we do contact some Cheyennes, maybe I can talk some sense into 'em with Elmira translating." He grinned. "Or maybe she can translate when I plead for them not to kill and scalp me."

"Take care of yourselves," Wilkins said as Tanner and Elmira trotted away. The half-breed and the Osage looked at each other, neither willing to express the fear that they would never see their two friends again.

CHAPTER 27

"You look like hell, Chase," Ralston said when Tanner and Cloud Dancer caught up with the small group.

"Two nights without sleep and plenty of hard ridin' will do that to a fella."

"You also look like you've been in a wrestling match with a bear."

"Me and Charlie had us a difference of opinion for a spell."

"It get solved?"

"Yep."

"He and his family all right?"

"Yes. They drove your boys off without harm to themselves. Charlie said he thinks they wounded two of the attackers."

"They ain't my boys, and I hope the two who were wounded have died on the trail."

"Wouldn't put me out none."

"There anyplace to bed down for the night? It's still mid-afternoon, but you and your woman look downright beat, and these

296

three," he pointed at the other men, "ain't much better. An early camp might do us all some good."

"There's another creek a few miles farther on if I recall correctly."

The rest did indeed do them all good, and they moved on with renewed spirits the next morning. As they rode, Ralston watched Tanner and finally rode up beside him.

"You seemed bothered, Chase. Something wrong?"

"I get the feelin' trouble ain't far off. You know how far it is to Bruckner's ranch?"

"I don't know my way around here, but judgin' by how far we've come and how far I've been told his place is, we can't be more than five, six miles."

"I got a bad feelin'. We best push on a bit faster."

Two hours later, they heard the faint sounds of gunfire. "That don't sound good," Ralston said.

"No, it don't, but I reckon it means at least some of the fools are alive. Let's ride!"

They raced off but slammed to a stop atop a small ridge that overlooked a spread of land that was empty except for a house up against the cottonwood-lined stream. It also held at least two dozen Indians. An almost equal number of white men were either in the house or using trees as protection near it.

"Looks even worse than it sounded," Ralston said. "What'll we do?"

"Hey there, Hayward, how's about you lead the charge down there to drive off those Indians you were so bent on killin'?" Disdain was thick in Tanner's voice.

Carl Hayward looked as if he were going to vomit, wet his trousers, faint, or all three.

"Didn't think so."

Ralston pointed at some Indians moving to get beyond the house and over the stream to come up behind the men hunkered down there.

"I see 'em." He looked around, then shrugged. "You boys think you can actually hit some Indians from here?" he asked, looking from Hayward to Downing to Hooper. The first's face was a mask of fright. The other two looked scared but determined. "Stake your horses a little way back, then settle yourselves in right here and start firing. Don't do it steady; take your time between shots. You send out a fusillade, they'll likely figure out where you are, and some of them will head your way. Firin' slowly will let the gun's smoke blow away, so it won't give away your position.

Just pick one or two off every now and again, and they might think bullets came from the trees."

The two nodded.

"You'll be all right?"

Both nodded again, seemingly afraid to talk.

"All right, Miles, let's go. Hayward, you can come or stay. Doesn't matter to me. Either way, keep out of the way and don't cause trouble."

They headed north, riding fast, aiming to get across the stream from this side and head off the warriors moving to get behind the white men.

Across the creek, they turned northeast. A hundred yards along, Tanner stopped them. He slid off his horse and grabbed his Spencer and a box of shells, which he stuffed into his shirt. "Take the horses and get behind that thicket there, Cloud." He and Ralston hurried forward.

Suddenly Tanner dropped to one knee, raised the rifle, and fired. A warrior went down. Whether the Indian was dead, Tanner did not know or care.

Seconds later, Ralston fired to his left. Another warrior went down.

Warriors were beginning to filter into the trees. Tanner and Ralston split and followed them. The former shot two more warriors, then saw another sneaking up on one of the defenders. With trees in the way, Tanner could not fire, so he charged forward and slammed into the Indian just before he splattered the white man's head with a tomahawk. The two rolled and Tanner came up first, shooting the warrior as he rose.

Glaring at the man he had just saved, Tanner said, "Indian lover, am I, Landis? Maybe I should've let him do his work."

"Thanks," Sid Landis squawked.

Then Tanner was gone again, stalking the woods. It seemed most of the warriors had fled and were on horseback, racing across the stream.

Tanner moved to the edge of the stream and began firing his repeating Spencer steadily. He noted that others kept up a steady fusillade from behind the trees. He assumed Ralston was one of those. He also saw an occasional puff of smoke from the low ridge and an occasional warrior go down.

Then the warriors were gone. Gunfire erupted from the log house, followed by cheers as men slowly came out into the open.

Suddenly Tanner heard a shot behind him and to his left, where he had left Cloud

Dancer. He ran that way, crashing through the underbrush. Ralston arrived a moment later. Tanner had stopped. Cloud Dancer had a smoking pistol, and Carl Hayward clutched a bloody arm.

"What happened, Cloud?" Tanner asked anxiously.

"He put hands on me, said he take me away. So I shoot."

"Good for you," Ralston said. "And you, Hayward . . ."

Before the former sergeant could say anything more, Tanner cut him off with a wave of the hand. He pulled his Colt. "I told you what would happen if you laid hands on my wife. I let Miles here talk me out of killin' you one time. He won't do it again." He cocked the revolver.

"Don't, Chase," Ralston said, though without fervor.

"I do," Cloud Dancer said.

"You sure?"

"Yes."

"It won't come back and make you have bad dreams?"

The Cheyenne smiled. "No."

"Then go on ahead." He didn't want to watch but had to. Ralston, he noticed, had turned away.

"I say before you bad man. I make sure

you not be bad man anymore."

"Don't, please!" Hayward screeched. "No, don't kill me. I promise I'll never . . ."

His pleas ended when a slug from Cloud Dancer's revolver punched a hole in his forehead.

Tanner glanced at Ralston, who had turned back around. "Looks like the Cheyennes got another one," he said with a smile.

Ralston looked shocked, then nodded.

The Cheyennes and Arapahos had killed seven whites. The whites killed at least a dozen warriors. One of the men gleefully said, "I aim to get me some souvenirs. How about you boys?"

"You take one step toward those dead warriors, and you'll be joinin' 'em in the Happy Huntin' Ground," Tanner said.

The man glared at him. "Ah, you're the Injun-lovin' fella who pissed and moaned about us takin' well-earned souvenirs from those savages at Sand Creek, ain't you?"

Tanner was surprised when Sid Landis stepped forward and pounded the man in the face, knocking him to the ground. Then he placed a booted foot on the man's neck. "You were sayin' something derogatory about Mr. Tanner?" he asked harshly.

"No," the man squawked.

302

"Good thing. If it weren't for Mr. Tanner and Sergeant Ralston, the rest of us likely would've been dead in a couple of days. Those Indians would've starved or burned us out while we kept wastin' ammunition firin' at them when they mostly stayed out of rifle range. Anyone wants to take on Mr. Tanner over this will have to face me."

"And me," Ralston said.

"And me," Downing added.

"And me," Hooper chimed in.

"Any arguments from any of you boys?" Landis asked. He didn't expect any and got none. "What's gonna . . . ."

One of the men yelled, "Indians!" and reached for his revolver.

In a heartbeat, three six-guns were aimed at him.

"She's an Indian, all right. Cheyenne, to be exact. She's also my wife."

Everyone calmed down.

"Now, as I was sayin', what's gonna happen is several of you men will gather up the Indians' bodies, take them out there beyond rifle range, and set them out nicely. We'll wrap 'em in blankets if we have 'em."

"What for?" Aaron Pitts asked, warily watching Tanner.

"Maybe they'll decide we ain't so bad after all if we don't abuse the bodies. Maybe they'll leave us all alone. Maybe not, but it's worth a try. If I catch any of you takin' so much as a fingernail from any of those warriors, I will shoot you myself."

"What if they don't like it?"

"Then we'll have another battle on our hands."

"What if they're a lot more of them, maybe hundreds?" another man asked.

"Then we have another big battle. Or run like hell. The Army's been out lookin' for these Indians. They ain't had much luck so far, but I sense they'll run these warriors down soon. Mr. Bruckner, I'd suggest you move on into Kiowa for a spell. Let things cool down here."

"I can't do that, Sid."

"I understand, but there'll be no more parties to come out here and help should you be attacked again." Landis looked around and began pointing at men. "You boys will get those warriors' bodies and do what I said." He pointed some more. "And you boys will find a suitable spot and bury our men. Whoever's left can start cookin' up something for the rest of us."

"What're you gonna be doin'?" Dan Atkins asked.

"Keepin' an eye on the rest of you. Now get to work."

■ ■ ■ ■

"You still thinkin' of movin' to Montana Territory, Chase?" Ralston asked. It was a couple of hours after he, Tanner, Cloud Dancer, Landis, and most of the other men had started back to Kiowa.

"Well, now that my reputation is intact again," Tanner said sarcastically, "me and Elmira might just stick around a while."

ABOUT THE AUTHOR

Though it might sound strange for someone who has published more than 60 westerns, **John Legg** was born and raised in New Jersey. An Air Force veteran, he has traveled much of the West, having been a newspaper copy editor for more than 27 years in Phoenix. He works for a major newspaper's editing center in Florida. He has a BA from William Paterson College (now university) in Wayne, N.J., and an MSJ from the Medill School of Journalism at Northwestern University. He has two grown children and two young grandsons.

The employees of Thorndike Press hope you have enjoyed this Large Print book. All our Thorndike, Wheeler, and Kennebec Large Print titles are designed for easy reading, and all our books are made to last. Other Thorndike Press Large Print books are available at your library, through selected bookstores, or directly from us.

For information about titles, please call:
(800) 223-1244

or visit our website at:
gale.com/thorndike

To share your comments, please write:
Publisher
Thorndike Press
10 Water St., Suite 310
Waterville, ME 04901